EVERYTHING LED
ME TO YOU

BY SARA KATE

COPYRIGHT

CHAPTER 1

The sound of the wind whirls through my ears as I drive with my windows down on Burr Oak Road. Even though my thin ponytail slaps my cheeks in the breeze, I'm enjoying the night drive. Autumn, which is my favorite season, just started here in Illinois, so the weather feels perfect out tonight. Since it's just twenty minutes past 11:00 p.m., I decided to take this back street to get to my best friend's apartment, because I wanted to avoid the busy Friday night traffic on the other streets.

I live in a suburban city called Forest Hill which is just an hour north outside of downtown Chicago, so the roads around here are normally busy no matter the time of day. Burr Oak Road barely ever has traffic on it though. It is a two-laned residential street, aligned by dense woods. The only light that is illuminating the road right now is coming from the headlights of my car. There aren't any signs, streetlights, or houses until I drive another half mile or so past the curve, which is only a few feet ahead of me.

There is a song playing on my radio, but it sounds annoyingly repetitive, so I think I'll change it... but I get distracted by the headlights in front of me.

They're bright and they're suddenly coming toward me fast.

They are so fast, that they begin to blind me.

Instinctually, I go to flash my high beams at the other driver.

But I'm too late.

The force from the other vehicle slamming head on into my car, sends me spinning uncontrollably and even though I'm wearing a seatbelt, my body is jolting everywhere in its seat.

I know I'm screaming, but I can't hear myself over the screeching sounds of my tires.

Everything is loud and out of my control.

I can't see the other vehicle's headlights anymore. *I can't see anything but darkness.*

I'm slamming on the brake pedal, but no matter how hard I step on it, my car just continues to keep wildly spinning, right before it slides down the side of the road and into the woods.

The White Room

I just opened my eyes to see a white ceiling in the distance above me. It's so high up that I can't see where it ends. I'm lying down on my back but I'm not sure on whose bed. It's not mine, that I know for sure because this bed feels like it is a lot stiffer and smaller than my own.

I don't know why I am laying down and I can't remember arriving here... I can't even recall what I was doing before this.

I am trying to lift my body to sit up, but my arms won't move. I think I'm being restrained against the bed because I can't move my body at all. I can only turn my head to the left and right, just enough to see that the walls around me are white, like the ceiling, but they also seem so far away that I can't tell where the room ends.

"Hello?" I call out as loud as I can, but no one answers me.

A moment passes before I attempt to sit up but then I feel someone touch my left arm. "Woah!" I gasp and quickly turn my head over to the left, but I don't see anyone.

But I felt a hand touch me just now... I know it.

I try to look down toward my arm, but I can't see it.

Is my neck being restrained too?

It's like I'm frozen to this bed or as if someone or something is holding me down, but I don't feel any pressure on me. I *did* feel someone's hand touch my arm though, I know that. *But why can't I see them? Where did they go?*

Panic is starting to set in and I only panic if my instincts tell me that I am about to be in trouble. I have low anxiety, but I believe that is because I have good intuition. Whenever I feel like something is wrong, I'm

3

usually right in some way and right now, I definitely feel like something is wrong because I've never felt so uncomfortable and confused in my life before.

I need to get the hell out of here, so that's what I'm going to do.

Just as I am trying to break free from the bed again, I get startled when I feel a hand touch my forehead. "AH! STOP!" I shriek but the hand stays on top of me.

I don't like that I can feel someone… but I can't see them.

"STOP!" I cry out again, but the hand is starting to massage my scalp and it's making me more and more uncomfortable. "Stop! I don't like this!" I'm practically pleading. "STOP! STOP TOUCHING ME!" I keep begging, but I don't think the person can hear me because now I feel fingers going through the roots of my hair.

Either they can't hear me, or they are purposely not listening to me and if that's the case, then that's starting to freak me out even more.

"STOP! STOP IT!"

There is another pair of hands gripping around the bicep of my right arm while the fingers are still running through my hair now.

I've never felt so violated and helpless before in my life. Why won't they stop touching me and why can't I see them?

My right arm is being lifted in the air now and I'm trying to resist but it's not working. I can't pull it away from the person's grip. They won't let go of me no matter how hard I try to pull my arm away.

"STOP! STOP! I DON'T LIKE THIS! GET YOUR HANDS OFF ME!"

No one is listening to me which is not only freaking me out even more but it's also starting to tremendously aggravate me. *I absolutely hate when no one listens to me.*

Fingertips continue to run through my scalp and down the strands of my forehead bangs. *It feels like these people are antagonizing me on purpose.*

I'm trying to struggle away but it's doing no good. "PLEASE! STOP! STOP TOUCHING ME!" I'm demanding through sobs and even though, I know that I'm crying, I don't feel any tears on my cheeks. *I just feel these random hands on me.*

My chest is starting to feel heavy, like someone is sitting on top of it. It sort of feels like I'm on the edge of a panic attack and that's not good at all. I've only ever had minor panic attacks, and this is how I can recall them starting. *I know this isn't a time for me to panic but damn, it's difficult not to do so.*

"PLEASE! STOP!" I yell out but still, no one is listening.

I've never felt like I have been tortured or tormented in any way before, but now I feel like I am, and I can't stand it. My mind is telling my body to fight and get myself out of here... *but how do I do that when I'm stuck like this?*

Finally, the hands left my hair, and my arm isn't lifted in the air anymore either. I need to close my eyes and control my breathing. If I can't feel my body and I can't see anything, I must be dreaming... or should I call it, a really fucked up nightmare. Now, all I have to do is figure out how to wake myself up from it.

CHAPTER 2

I'm not inside of the white room anymore. I can tell because I can hear distant beeping sounds and I can also feel my body now. *Every* muscle and bone ache unbearably. I didn't feel any pain when I was in the white room except for extreme discomfort when someone was touching me, but thankfully no one is touching me right now. I am still lying on my back, but I'm not on the same bed that I was laying on in the white room and it's definitely still not my own bed in my apartment either.

The beeping sounds are starting to get louder as the pain in my body elevates and it's really scaring me. *I know that I need to open my eyes right now but I'm too afraid…*

"Jen, Jen, it's okay. We're here. It's okay…"

Is that my mom's voice?

"Jen, it's okay sweetie. We're here."

That's my dad too! Good! If they're here, then that means I'm safe now and I can open my eyes.

"Jen?" My mom and dad both say my name almost in unison as soon as my eyes meet theirs.

Now I know what the beeping sounds are. I'm lying on my back while slightly sitting up in a hospital bed. The hospital gown that I'm wearing is twice the size of me and I have two blankets draped over the lower half of my body. The blankets are heavy over my knees when I go to shift my legs. I start to examine my body and look down to my right arm first because it feels notably heavier than my left and I realize that it's in a cast.

That means I broke it but that's confusing because I've never broken anything on my body before and I don't remember what I was doing to break it.

"Jen," Mom has been repeatedly saying my name now, but I haven't answered because I've been too busy being pre-occupied with examining my body.

It's mine but it doesn't feel that way.

"Mom... Dad," I say slowly as I look at them and they both just busted out into tears. I think they are happy tears because my mom is holding her hands over her chest like she is relieved. "What happened? How did I break my arm?" I ask as I look at my cast.

My dad grabs hold of my left hand. The look on his face is bewildering to me. I've never seen him look like this. "You don't remember what happened at all?" he asks.

I shake my head no, which sends a shooting pain through the nape of my neck and up the back of my head.

"Take it slow," he says as I let go of his hand and go to sit myself up more. The pain is excruciating in my lower back when I sit up. It feels like my back has a large bruise on it when I rest against the pillows.

I'm glad I can feel all of my body but when I begin to touch my face, I stop when my fingers graze over stitches on my forehead under my bangs. I move my palm from there and through the roots of my hair. Then I feel around to the back of my head, but I stop when I feel more stitches just above the nape of my neck. I look at my dad. "What happened to me?"

"You were in a car accident, honey. You have a small stitch on your forehead and a another one just above your neck," he tells me. "Just take it slow. The nurse or doctor should be here any second."

*I last remember being in the white room but before that...
I can only slightly recall seeing bright lights when I was
driving... I don't remember the accident happening though.*

"I think I saw the headlights of a car, but I-- I don't
think I can remember the accident actually happening. I
was driving to Michelle's," I pause when I think about the
white room. "Wait, was I just asleep? There was a room...
It was white. Someone kept touching me," I shake my
head. "I'm confused."

My dad exchanges a worried look from me to my mom
and then back at me before he says, "you weren't asleep,
Jen. You were in a coma for the past week."

—

Question after question after question. *Do you know
your name? Do you know your age? What is your birthdate?
What is the last thing you remember doing?*

The list went on. I have never been asked so many
questions about myself by a doctor or really by anyone
until just a little over half an hour ago. After giving
answers to all the questions that I already had my
answers to, my doctor told me that I sustained a
traumatic brain injury during the car accident which is
what sent me into a mild coma. When my car got hit, it
spun off the side of the road and slid down a small ditch
leading into the woods and landed head on into a tree.

According to what my doctor said, I went into a coma
due to the impact of the airbag that deployed out of my
steering wheel. Even though the airbag came out as it
should have, it did not soften the impact of the crash for
me. Instead, it did the exact opposite. Because I am on the
shorter side in height, (I am only 5'1), the airbag not only

smacked me in the face more aggressively than it would on most adults, but it also made my head bounce back against the headrest causing my brain to suffer from so much bruising and swelling, that I got knocked out and sent into a coma.

After hearing all of that, I spent a good minute exchanging an unbelievable stare between both my doctor and my parents because everything that I had just been told simply didn't match my memory. I'm very grateful that I didn't lose any recollection of who I am after being practically dead for a whole week, but I'm really upset that I can't remember the accident itself. It all happened so quickly that I don't even recall what the other vehicle looked like or the moment that it smashed into me.

Oddly though, as I sit here and try to think back to driving on Burr, I can now only remember before and in between the crash. I know that I was approaching the curve when I saw the headlights. It was like they just appeared out of nowhere. Then the next thing I knew, I felt my car spinning. I don't even remember the other vehicle initially hitting me first, or my car landing in the woods. I do remember everything about the white room when I was in my coma though, and I wish it is the one thing I could forget. *I hated being in that room. I couldn't move.*

I asked my doctor why that was happening to me, and she told me that I was probably feeling that way whenever I was being touched by someone in real life. Whether it was the doctor, nurses, my parents, or my friends who were touching my body in the hospital, my brain didn't know or couldn't tell me what was going on, so I guess it scared me when I was in the white room.

Understanding that, began to set my mind at ease until a police officer just walked into my room right now. She looks to be about an inch or two taller than me. Her skin tone is a shade tanner than my olive skin, and she has tight brunette curls which are tied back into a low ponytail. As she stands with a notebook in her hands, her face is tense.

"Hello, Jen. I am Officer Rodriguez. I am assigned to your case," she says in a dry tone that matches her face.

"My case?" I question.

"Yes," she nods. "Since the driver of the vehicle that crashed into you fled the scene, we opened a hit and run case. I am hoping that you can provide us with some information to help us find who it was."

"Uh, w--what?" I stutter as I look over at my parents. They told me that I was in an accident, but they didn't get as far as telling me that the person drove away from it.

"I'm sorry, honey. We didn't want to overwhelm you with everything right away," my dad says as soon as his eyes meet mine.

I look back toward Officer Rodriguez. "So, you're telling me that the person who almost killed me hasn't been caught yet? You don't have *any* clues?"

"No. I'm sorry ma'am. I do not have any leads yet. I was hoping that you can help me by telling me what you can remember the night of your accident though. Do you remember what the vehicle looked like?"

"I-I don't know. I can't remember much. The last thing I remember seeing were the headlights," I pause as I think about the moment leading up to the crash. "I remember that I wanted to change the radio station but then the headlights distracted me when I was about to drive around the curve."

"So, you weren't looking at the road when it happened?" she asks as she starts writing and I am blindsided by her question.

"Uh, what? No, that's not what I meant," I scrunch my forehead in confusion. "I was looking at the road. I just meant; that was the last thing I can remember right before I saw the lights coming toward me," I say and then I give my parents an odd look. They both look confused too.

"Okay, and when you saw these headlights, did they look like they were higher up than your car? Do you remember if maybe they were on a bigger vehicle, like a truck?" Officer Rodriguez asks.

"Honestly, I really don't know. It happened so quickly," I mumble.

If the cops were waiting on me to give them information about this person, then that's not a good sign because I can't remember shit about the vehicle except those damn headlights.

"Okay, ma'am. We will be in touch if I need anything further," she says as she closes her notebook. "I will leave you my card if you have any questions."

"No, wait," I stop her. "So, you mean to tell me that no one saw anything at all? How is that possible? This city isn't that *huge*. I mean, someone had to see or hear something."

"We questioned the neighbors in the area, but no one reported anything," Officer Rodriguez says as she starts pulling out her card to hand to me. I can tell that she does not want to be here, but I don't care how she feels, because I don't want to be here either.

"So, who made the 911 call then?" I question while I don't take her card.

"Another driver made the call. They saw your car off the side of the road a few minutes after your accident happened," she answers.

"How do you know it was a few minutes after it happened?" I groan in agony when I cross my arms against my torso because the muscles in my upper back ache when I move.

"Because the paramedics told me that if you didn't get medical attention within the ten minutes after your accident, then you would have been in a lot worse of a condition," Officer Rodriquez answers in a way where I can tell that she is trying her best to not look or sound annoyed. *However, she is not doing a great job at masking it.*

"Well, who was the person that found me then? How do you know it wasn't them who crashed into me?"

"Because they provided their name on the phone, they waited for the paramedics to arrive, and their car was intact, ma'am. If I get anything new that comes up, I promise that I will contact you. Until then, here is my card." She leaves her card beside me on the bed and walks out of the room.

I look at my parents dumbfounded. "That was it?"

"Jen, you need to rest for now. I'm sure the cops will figure it out," my mom says as she gets up from the chair and sits on the side of my hospital bed.

Rest? How can I rest after what I just heard? Someone almost killed me, and they are still out there, while here I am - laying in a hospital bed with an injured brain, stitches, a broken arm, and a week of my life taken away from me. I know it was late when it happened at night, but someone had to have seen or heard something around here. *It's not fair that I had to put my life on hold, and that other driver didn't. They're the ones that crashed*

12

into me and I'm going to do my best to find out who the hell they are.

CHAPTER 3

After I awoke out of my coma, my doctor kept me in the hospital for a whole week before she finally discharged me to go back home. When she did, my parents refused to let me go back to my apartment by myself and I didn't try to argue with them. This is my first time I am living on my own. I moved out of my parent's apartment and into my own a few days after I turned nineteen and that was only five months ago. I am an only child which means my parents are still getting used to my new independence, so letting them stay with me for the past six days was more for their own sake than mine. It wasn't until this morning when I finally convinced them that I was fine, and they ended up leaving.

Now, I am on my way to Forest Hill's community college so I can sign up to start classes next semester. I was supposed to do this just two days after my accident happened, but I obviously didn't get the chance since I was lying unconscious in a hospital bed. As I drive to the campus, I fumble through my purse with my casted arm to look for my cell phone. I've never had a broken arm before and if I could've chosen which one to break, I would have definitely chosen the one that I don't use for everything. I wait until I get to a stoplight so I can dial Officer Rodriguez's number.

I've called her only once since I last saw her because I

want an update, but she didn't have any new information to give me. It's been three days since then, so I'm hoping she will tell me that she finally has a lead.

"Forest Hill police," a woman that does not sound like Officer Rodriguez answers.

"Hello. I am calling to talk to Officer Rodriguez," I say.

"She's busy at the moment, Can I help you?"

"I'm calling to check on case 6875," I answer.

"What is your name?"

"Jennifer Russo."

"And what are you calling in regards about it?"

"I'd like to know if you have any new details regarding who the suspect might be," I try to answer her without sounding irritated.

Why else would I be calling about it?

After a few seconds of silence, she comes back on the phone and says, "No, ma'am. I do not see anything new here in your report."

"Nothing at all?" I ask in disbelief.

"No ma'am, nothing new," she repeats.

"Uh, alright, thanks," I sigh. I don't put up a fight and end the call as I pull into the school's parking lot. I'll just call back Officer Rodriguez again tomorrow. I don't have enough time to argue right now. I really don't even know what to argue about. I just know that I want the driver that crashed into me to get caught and I am going to make sure the police are fully aware of that.

As I get out of my car, I text my best friend, Michelle to let her know that I am here. Unlike me, she's been in college for almost a year now since she enrolled in the fashion program only a few months after we graduated high school. I didn't enroll right away because I wasn't sure about what I wanted to do for a career yet. I'm not passionate about fashion, like Michelle and I don't have any real hobbies either. It wasn't until just two months ago when I decided that I was going to pursue a career as a middle school language arts teacher. I only chose teaching because I've always been good in grammar, and it beats customer service which I am sadly in right now. I've been working as a front desk receptionist at a salon for two years and it has made me realize that I am not prepared or willing to spend the rest of my life as one.

I'm not too excited to be a teacher yet, but I think I rather work with children as opposed to working with adults if I have the choice. I'm sure that if I don't like teaching, then I can switch my major but I'm not delaying the enrollment process any longer. I fear that if I wait too long to enroll, then I will never do it because I'll just end up pushing it off.

Michelle just texted me back. She told me that her class is getting out in five minutes and to meet her in front of the bulletin board by the entrance. I need her to show me where the administration office is, since I've only been here one other time for a tour, and I don't remember. The campus isn't huge, but it has four buildings, and I don't feel like roaming around the hallways when I can have her just show me where it is.

The breeze is extra strong today and it's making my bangs blow back into my hair which is slightly aggravating. I cut my hair into eyebrow length bangs only a month prior to my accident and I've regretted it from the moment I was done cutting. I'm not entirely sure what I was thinking when I decided to do it. I mean, it *might have been* because I was dealing with a breakup from my first boyfriend, but I rather not fully admit to that theory. If I did, then that would just be another thing that I let my ex take from me.

As I approach the board, I begin to pull up my brunette hair into a high ponytail but it's difficult with my broken arm. Since my hair is so thin and straight, strands are always falling out and they keep getting caught inside of my cast. I've mastered being able to drive with this thing on my arm easier than putting up my hair, go figure. While I am struggling with the wind, my purse slides off my left shoulder and on to the ground. At the same time, I hear a male's voice which sort of startles me.

"Are you going tonight?" he asks, and I turn to see a man nearly towering over me as he is at least six feet tall. He has a folder in one hand and my purse in the other. His deep brown eyes glisten when he smiles which I immediately get taken back by. He has an athletic body type, not too muscular but it's obvious that he works out. I can tell because his lean muscles are popping through his tight black crew neck T-shirt. He hands me my purse as I look at him, perplexed. "Uh, what? Going where?" I ask.

He gestures toward the board, then I notice he is looking at a party flyer. "Oh, uh… no, I'm not going. I actually don't go here yet," I say as I shake my head while I hang my purse on my left shoulder. "I'm just waiting to meet my friend so she can take me to admissions."

"Oh, I just enrolled myself," he says as he holds up the folder which reads the words FOREST HILL COMMUNITY in capital letters.

"What a coincidence," I smile as I awkwardly pull some lose strands of my hair out from the inside of my cast. I am taken back by how handsome this man is. He has a buzzcut which I find oddly attractive since I normally like guys with long hair. He also has a goatee and a mustache which I don't normally find attractive on many guys, but for some reason, I think it looks good on him.

"JEN!" I hear Michelle calling my name from across the campus and I widen my eyes in embarrassment as I look past this guy's shoulder to see her waving her hand in the air from the other hallway. He turns around to see what I'm looking at and chuckles.

"That's my best friend," I sigh. "I better go meet her. It was nice meeting you."

"Good luck with enrollment," he smiles, and I politely nod, then I walk toward Michelle as he heads toward the parking lot.

"Who was that?" Michelle immediately asks when I approach her.

"I don't know. Some guy," I shrug.

"The side of his face looked hot. Did you get his number?" She steps on her tip toes to look in the direction of which way he walked. Michelle is the complete opposite of me in many aspects. She is a bleach blonde pin straight, long haired five-foot-tall woman who only weighs a little over ninety pounds. While she is more of a petite thin stick figure, I am ten pounds heavier, curvier, and a whole bra size bigger than her. I also have about a quarter less confidence than she does because she is extremely outgoing and has high self-esteem. She's not only confidently loud but she speaks her mind all the time, which can be a good or a bad thing. It depends on the situation.

"You know I don't just get guys numbers like that. I'm not you," I laugh and roll my eyes while I follow her down one of the hallways. My cell rings in my purse and I pull it out to see that the caller I.D. is from the bank of where I took a loan out for my now totaled car.

"Hello?" I answer.

"Hello, I'm looking to speak with Jennifer Russo. My name is Allie. I am calling from the bank about the loan on your scion."

"Oh, yes. Is everything okay?" I answer.

"You are a month behind on the payment for your Toyota. I am calling to see if you would like to pay anything today or set up a different plan if you're starting to have trouble with making the payments?"

"Um," I hesitate, "My car got totaled weeks ago in the accident. I thought I didn't have to make any more payments. I don't even have the car anymore."

"We did get the payment from the insurance company but since you did not have any gap insurance, you still have to pay off the remaining balance for your car," Allie answers and I stop walking. I still owe a little over four thousand dollars to the dealership, but I thought that I wouldn't have to still pay that after my car got totaled.

"So," I pause, "you're telling me that I still owe about four thousand dollars on a car that I don't even have anymore?"

Michelle's mouth just dropped open as she stops walking and looks back at me.

"No, ma'am," Allie answers. "Your insurance took care of what your car was worth which was $3,000 after the deductible but you still owe the remainder, which is one thousand dollars, so you have a couple more payments that you still owe."

"Wait, what is gap insurance?" I ask. "I didn't know I needed that. I've never even heard of that."

"Gap insurance protects you from car depreciation. Vehicles decrease in value once they are bought. Gap insurance is offered to cover your car if it gets totaled or stolen. Since you owe more than the cars depreciated value and you didn't have gap, you owe what is left. If you had the gap insurance added to your policy, then you wouldn't owe anything. It would have covered it for you."

"Uh, uh… okay," I sigh as I try to understand what she just told me but truthfully, I have no idea what she just explained. "Well, I never knew about gap insurance. I don't think I was ever even offered when I signed up for my insurance."

A moment passes before Allie responds, "I'm very sorry, ma'am."

I am almost speechless right now. I just figured that since my car was gone, then the money owed should be gone too, but I guess I was wrong.

"Uh, ok, thanks. I'll make a payment online soon," I sigh as I have really nothing to say or neither the energy to argue.

"Did I just hear you right? Your car is totaled. Why would you still owe the money?" Michelle asks when I end the call.

"Because I didn't have something called gap insurance." I roll my eyes. "You know, every day since I woke up from my coma, something new aggravates me. I just want my life back to normal," I groan as I feel my eyes get teary. Before my accident, I never got emotional this easily but lately it seems like everything is just too hard to handle and the littlest inconveniences make me want to cry.

Michelle gives me a half smile. "I don't think your life is going to be normal for a while Jen, but it *will* get back to normal. You will be fine, I promise. At least you are alive and standing here in one piece right now. We will find whoever hurt you. I know you're mad because I'm mad at that asshole too but right now, let's forget about everything and try to look forward."

I stop walking to give her a perplexing look. Michelle isn't the type to speak in such an uplifting way. We both aren't. We've been friends since elementary school. Not only do we equally have dry senses of humor, but we're both naturally sarcastic which is probably why we've been such close friends for so long.

"When did you become so full of wisdom?" I put my hands on my hips.

"I was reading a lot of positivity quotes when you were dead for a week," she smirks. "What did you say that the insurance was called that you needed?"

"Apparently, something called gap insurance. Never heard about it or was offered." I shrug.

"Hmm, I think I need to check my cars insurance policy then," she says.

I look at her and we both laugh as we approach the building with the admissions office.

—

I was able to successfully enroll for classes yesterday which lifted my mood up after the phone call about my loan. Although I wasn't expecting to still pay for my nonexistent car, I decided to not let that ruin my day and I still finished the enrollment process. After that, I went back home and just relaxed for the rest of the day since my apartment is now parent free.

It's 8:00 AM and I just woke up about half an hour ago. I don't have any plans today because I am off work so I think I'll go take a walk to Stoney's diner which is only a couple blocks over, that way I can get some coffee. I can make coffee here, but I've been craving my usual caramel Frappuccino from Stoney's and I haven't had one in a few weeks. Before I leave though, I am calling Officer Rodriguez to check on my case.

"Forest Hill Police. How can I assist you?" Instead of Officer Rodriguez answering the phone, it sounds like the same woman that answered when I called yesterday.

"Hi. How are you? My name is Jen. I am calling to get an update on a car accident that happened a few weeks ago. It was a hit-"

"Yes, yes. I know who you are," she immediately cuts me off in a clearly agitated tone.

"Ma'am, I spoke to you yesterday. I'm sorry but there's still nothing new," she answers in an exasperated tone.

She says that she's sorry, but she doesn't sound it.

"An officer that is assigned to your case will call you whenever they have more information. If no one has called yet, then there is no new information," she says.

Deep breaths, I remind myself. I am trying to stay calm, but her tone isn't making it easy for me. "Yes, I do understand that…" I exhale. "But can you at least tell me what procedure you're taking? No one-"

"Ma'am, I'm sorry. I do not have anything more to tell you about the case right now. We will give you a call when we have something," she says and before I know it the phone call is over.

Out of frustration, I slam my left palm against my kitchen counter which regrettably stings. Holding back tears, I shut my eyes for a moment while I take some deep breaths.

I can't let this ruin my day right now. I want to enjoy my last day off before I go back to work tomorrow. I throw on a plain dark purple hoodie over my tank top and a pair of ripped blue jeans. Then I slip my feet into my black ankle boots before I throw up my hair into a messy high bun. I didn't wash my hair in the shower this morning or bother to really brush it so the messy bun look will have to do today.

I walk out of my door, lock it behind me and then I head down the first floor and out of the front entrance of my apartment building. As I begin my ten-minute walk over to Stoney's, my phone vibrates in my back jean pocket.

As I expected, I see that it's my mother calling when I go to answer. "Hi, mom."

"How are you feeling?"

"Not dead yet," I respond.

I hear her sigh loudly on the other end for a second before she ignores my comment and says, "where are you? I can hear wind."

"I am walking to Stoney's to get a frappe."

"Oh, can I meet you?" she asks. My parents live in a two-bedroom apartment on the other end of the city. It's not even a fifteen-minute drive away from me.

"Mom, you were with me for a whole week," I laugh. "I'm just going to pick up my coffee really quick and then rest for the day before I go back to work tomorrow."

"Okay. Well, call me if you need anything. Oh, how is the car driving? Dad said to let him know if the beamer starts sputtering again."

My dad is letting me borrow his old BMW sedan for now. It's about twelve years old and almost all the red paint has come off the hood. Now that I have to pay off my car, it's going to take me longer to get a new vehicle so until then, I guess I will be using the old beamer. It normally shakes every time you reach a speed over forty miles per hour. My dad wants me to tell him if it sputters but he won't be able to do anything about it because he can't afford to fix it.

My mom is a waitress, and my father is a cook. They've been working at an Italian restaurant in town for almost ten years now and they don't have any extra money to put into the beamer which is why it's been sitting in front of their apartment for the past year.

"It's driving fine so far. I only drove it to the college yesterday after you guys left. I'll let him know if it acts up," I answer. "Well, I'm about to walk into the diner. I'll talk to you later."

"Okay. I'm so excited for you to start college, honey! I'm so proud of you. Call me if you need anything. Love you," she says, emphasizing on the words *call me* again and I end the call as I walk through the entrance of the diner.

Stoney's is a small 24/7 diner located in a small outdoor strip mall that is stuck in between a barbershop and a clothing boutique. Although the diner resembles a bit of an old fashioned 1950's vibe on the outside, despite their attempt at designing the booths in a fifty's era fashion, the rest of the diner is surprisingly modern inside. There are various picture frames of all types of musicians throughout history decorated on the white interior walls. Silver leather booths which match the tables, line the walls under the photos.

I step into the door and sit down on the tall black bar stool at the counter in front of the kitchen. Once I do, I shockingly see the man that I met at school yesterday. He walks out from the kitchen while wearing a red Stoney's T-shirt and black apron on his waist over his jeans.

He flashes me the same wide smile he did yesterday when he notices me, "Hey! Uh, remember me? We met yesterday morning at the school. My name is Max."

"Oh, hi. I'm surprised you remember meeting me," I say

in a baffled way. "We talked for like two seconds…"

"Well, it's kind of hard to forget a pretty face like yours," he shrugs, and I shyly giggle as I am realizing now that I may not know how to flirt.

Guys rarely hit on me and if they do, well most of the time it is normally because I am with Michelle. I know I am pretty, but I don't normally get hit on the way Max is hitting on me… if that is even what he's doing.

"Uh, thank you," I chuckle. I can feel my face growing hot.

"Can I get you something? You're actually not sitting in my section but since I'm here," he shrugs.

"I'll just take a small caramel Stoney's frappe in a to go cup, please."

Why did I say Stoney's? It's not like there'd be another type of frappe here.

"Gotcha. I'll be back," he responds and turns to go make my frappe.

Just a few minutes later, I hear Max's voice and I look up from my cell phone to see him placing my drink on the counter in front of me. I take it and thank him before I take a sip. "Mm! Oh my god! I forgot how much I missed this," I say with my eyes closed, still savoring the caramel taste in my mouth.

"Good?" he chuckles with a raised eyebrow.

"Uh, yeah," I put my drink down and try to hide my embarrassment. "I haven't had one of these in a while. I used to stop in here all the time before-" I stop myself from saying that I was nearly dead in a coma and instead I say, "I decided to start saving my money and stop eating out so much but… uh, I don't think I've ever seen you here. That is, when I used to come in."

Shit, I can feel my face getting red.

"Oh, well I just started working here," he smiles. "This is my second day on the floor by myself."

"Excuse me, is anyone coming over to this table?" a customer who is sitting at a booth in the back of the diner calls out to Max, and it makes me feel sort of relieved.

"Shit, uh, I should probably go do my job," Max lightly laughs as he gestures with his pointer finger to tell the man, *one moment.*

"Yeah, I don't want to be the reason you get fired," I smile.

"Eh, I think it'd be worth it." He winks at me right before he goes to walk out from behind the counter, but he stops himself before going to the customer and looks at me. "Hey, I know we just met but would you like to go out to dinner with me Friday night?"

Well, that wasn't something I was expecting, especially as I'm sipping on my coffee.

Flustered and unsure of what to say, I try not to stutter or spit my coffee out when I answer, "uh, yeah... sure. That-- that'd be nice. Oh, um... my name is Jen by the way."

Max's pearly whites shine when he laughs. "Oh yeah, I already knew that. I think the whole campus knew your name."

It takes me a quick second before I realize that he is talking about Michelle. She called my name from at least fifty feet away. "That's my best friend for you," I sigh.

As Max laughs again, he pulls out a notepad from his apron and rips off a blank piece of paper. "It's starting to get busy here. Leave your number on the counter before you go, and I'll pick it up after I'm done with my tables."

"Hello? Are you coming over here or not?" the same customer calls out in a more aggravated tone this time.

"Okay, I should get back to work. I can't get fired now... I need to be able to afford our date," he gives a slight chuckle and even though his line was off-guardingly cheesy, he made it sound oddly sexy. "I'll text you later," he says and goes to walk toward the customer.

"Oh wait, what about my check?" I stop him.

"Don't worry about it. It's on me," he smiles, then heads over to the customer.

Something about Max's persona is intriguing to me. I'm not used to guys being so forward with me like he just was. I never even felt as flustered as I just did in front of a guy before - not even my ex-boyfriend.

Without taking any more time to think about what just happened, I write with my left hand a hopefully readable phone number next to my name with a very uneven heart on the paper he left me. *Does the heart count as flirting or does that make me seem desperate?*

Either way, I already drew it. I take the remainder of my frappe with me and go toward the exit as the morning crowd starts to roll in. Right before I leave, I catch Max glance over my way from across the dining room and we both smile at each other before I walk out of the door.

CHAPTER 4

The only good thing that I can say about going into my coma was missing out on a week of dealing with this heavy, itchy cast on my arm. After five weeks of it being on, I am finally getting it taken off this morning. Michelle is on her way over to my apartment right now so she can go with me to my appointment. My mom offered to go with me, but I declined since her anxiety will just elevate mine. I still don't want to go alone though so I'm taking Michelle. I also don't want to risk the beamer shaking on the way there if I don't have too.

As I'm putting on a light blue long sleeve, my phone rings and I see that it's Officer Rodriguez. I hit the answer button so quick that I nearly drop the phone out of my hand.

"Hello?" I ask eagerly.

"Can I speak with Jennifer Russo, please? This is officer Rodriguez."

"This is her. Do you have new information on who crashed into me?" I gasp.

I am way too anxious.

"No, I am very sorry. We do not have any new information, ma'am," she says. "I'm actually calling to tell you that we are closing the case today."

My mouth just fell open. *Did I just hear her right? Close my case when this person is still out there?*

"Uh, I-I, wait, hold on. There's got to be... just... hold on! Don't close it yet!" I can barely speak in a full coherent sentence.

"I'm sorry, but we've kept your case open for longer than we should have. Unfortunately, there is nothing more we can do," she answers.

Again, she says she is sorry, but she doesn't sound it.

"Nothing more you can do? "I repeat in angst. "Are you kidding me? I almost died..."

"Ma'am, I understand you went through a traumatic experience, but I really wish I could help more. Unfortunately, I have no leads on who the other driver might be," she answers which just irritates me more.

I take a deep breath as I feel my eyes tear up. In a shaky voice I manage to scowl the words, "ugh, uh... okay. Thanks for nothing! You guys are fucking garbage!" I end the call and throw my phone onto my couch.

Why did she have to call and tell me that now? First thing in the morning. Today was supposed to be the first day of getting back to my normal life; getting my cast off and going back to work. I was in a good mood up until now. I take a few minutes to pace around the four-foot square wooden coffee table in my living room before I decide that I'm calling Officer Rodriguez back. There's got to be something else she can do.

When I pick my phone up from off the couch, I get distracted by an unread text message from Max. He sent it only a minute ago, but I didn't hear my phone buzz. It reads - **Morning Jen!** *Looking forward to tonight. I'll pick you up at 8:00 p.m.*

In the moment, I forget about the phone call with Officer Rodriguez and all I can do is picture Max's face. I text back- **Good morning! Can't wait!**

As I hit send, I feel the corners of my mouth just slightly rise up to my cheeks when I smile.

"Bitch, why is your door unlocked?" Michelle cursing at me from my doorway suddenly distracts me. She is standing in silver four-inch heel, knee high boots which match her long-sleeved dark purple V-Neck dress. I was too busy thinking about Max, that I did not even hear my door open. "Are you asking for someone to come murder you?" She crosses her arms at her torso. Count on Michelle to always be my bodyguard. Even though she's small, her personality isn't.

"Relax. I left it unlocked for you since I knew you were coming," I laugh. "Cute outfit."

"I got to stay stylish if I'm going to be a stylist." She twirls around but stops when she notices my face. "Wait, what's wrong? Why do you look like that?" she asks with concern. If anyone knows me well besides my parents, it's Michelle. I don't have a good poker face around her.

"The cops closed my case," I roll my eyes and plop myself on the couch, emotionlessly. "I don't want to talk about it. There's some coffee left if you want any before we leave."

She sits down next to me. "I had some already. When did you find this out?"

"Literally, just a few minutes ago. I got the call right before you walked in. I was about to call Officer Rodriguez back, but I got distracted when I saw Max's text," I sigh.

Michelle drops her decorative nonprescription bug-eyed reading glasses to the tip of her nose. She widens her eyes. "WHO?"

I tell her about how I coincidentally met Max at the diner after meeting at the school, and she is absolutely thrilled. "I would've taken notice to a face like his at

Stoney's before. We know, like, almost every server there. How long has he been working there? Where are you going for your date?"

She's immediately starting with the questions.

"First of all, you said you only saw the side of his face and that was for like, a few seconds, so you don't even know what he looks like." I roll my eyes. "But he did say he just started working there so that's probably why we never seen him, and I have no clue where he's taking me. He just asked me out for dinner, and I agreed."

"Hmm, this sounds like fate to me! What's his handle?" she asks as she pulls her phone out from her purse.

"I don't think he has social media. If he does, I haven't found him yet. I already tried to look him up. I'll just ask him when I see him again," I answer.

Her mouth drops. "No social media? Do we think that's a good or bad thing?"

"I don't know," I shrug my shoulders. "I didn't even know that I was going to say yes when he asked me out. I got awkwardly nervous, and I just agreed. I didn't even think about it," I sigh. "He's really hot, but I'm not sure I should be dating right now. That's really been the last thing on my mind lately."

As I finish my sentence, my phone rings between us and I rush to pick it up. I'm hoping that it's Officer Rodriguez calling to say she made a mistake or something… but instead, it's my mom. "Ugh," I groan while I mute the ringer. "I can't answer her right now."

"You know what? Screw the police," Michelle says as she springs up from the couch. "Forget about those useless assholes. Let's get that cast off you, so you don't have to be broken for your date with Max."

I am still sitting here slumped against the cushion as

she's standing with her hands on her hips in front of me. "Come on," she pulls me by my hands, and I reluctantly sit up. "I know you been through a lot but now, you have something to be excited for, Jen. The first step in getting back to your normal life is getting this gaudy purple thing off your arm."

I look her up and down with raised eyebrows. "Those positivity quotes you were reading really spoke to you, huh?"

"Well, you were basically dead for a week, and no one knew if you were going to wake up so… yes. I guess you could say they did help. Now, let's go! Get up!"

"Okay. you're right," I reluctantly mumble as I look down at my purple cast and try to remind myself that I should be excited for this.

—

As I look at the designer holes in my blue jeans around my knees through my full-length mirror, I realize that I have no idea how to dress for a first date. I don't like to dress up and I've never been on an actual real first date before. I only had one boyfriend; Nate, and we did not start our relationship off like a normal couple. We were best friends for two years during high school before our friendship ended up turning into a relationship during senior year. After hanging out with our friends one night, Nate kissed me in his car right before he dropped me off at home and from there everything changed between us. He never formally asked me to be his girlfriend after that, but our friends eventually noticed us flirting and before we knew it, we were deemed a couple, and I guess we became okay with it.

So, in a traditional sense, I have never had a real first

date experience. I never really even thought about how a first date would go but I also never thought that I would experience one while I have a broken arm… or while I'm in the middle of recovering from a coma - *not that I ever imagined either of those things would happen to me.*

It's already 7:50 PM. Max should be here any minute to pick me up and I still don't have a shirt on. Even though these jeans are cute, I probably should not go for such a casual look. I don't have a classy shirt to match them and after all, Max did say he was taking me out to dinner. He didn't tell me that he's taking me to a fancy restaurant, but I should probably wear something a bit more in between casual and formal just in case. I wanted to have Michelle come help me get ready, but she wouldn't have made it here in time after getting off work so I'm on my own with this decision tonight.

I rummage through my closet and find a black knit A- line dress with a V-neck long sleeve that reaches just before my knees. I normally don't like dresses, but I know it fits me good because I bought it only a few months ago with Michelle. I didn't have a black dress before then and as Michelle likes to say; *a woman will need a black dress at least once in her life,* and I guess she was right. That time must be now.

I put it on and look down at my bare feet, knowing that she would tell me to wear high heels but instead, I decide to choose my black knee high one-inch heel boots. I think I've worn high heels once in my life which was for a friends quinceanera and that was two years ago. Just as I begin to apply an extra layer of foundation over the scar on my forehead, I hear a knock on my door and my heart instantly starts to race.

"Uh, one minute!" I call out in this overly high-pitched

voice that I've never heard come out of me. I quickly apply some more foundation on my face and then I touch up my oily cheeks with some powder.

When I open my front door, Max is standing there in a blue collared polo T-shirt with a light grey nylon jacket over it. He is wearing a pair of dark denim jeans that fit just right, not too baggy or too tight on him. He knows how to dress, stylish yet casual, just like his personality. "Nice to see you again. You look beautiful," he says as he reaches in to hug me.

I catch a whiff of his cologne and I have to hold myself back from nuzzling my nose in his neck when I wrap my arms around him. "Thank you," I say as I pull back from our hug.

"So, where are we going to eat?" I ask as I follow him out of my building and toward his silver SUV in the parking lot.

"There is a really nice restaurant called Avery's in South Townshed. I guess you could call it waterfront dining because it has a lakeview setting," he chuckles as he holds open the passenger side door for me. "Have you been?"

"Thank you," I say as I sit in the passenger seat. "Uh no, I haven't been there. I barely go to Townshed." Townshed is only about a twenty-five to thirty-minute drive away from Forest Hill, but I rarely ever need to go there. The town is more rural and less populated than Forest.

"I thought, we'd have some dinner there," Max says when he gets in the driver's seat and turns on the engine. "It's a tropical themed restaurant right when you get into town. The whole vibe of the place makes you think you're somewhere like Florida... or Hawaii." He looks over at me and smiles before putting the gear into drive. "We can pretend like the lake is a beautiful tropical beach."

"That sounds good," I agree and smile back. "I've never been to a real beach or anywhere tropical anyway."

"Really? Never?!" he gasps.

"Nope. Never," I laugh as I raise my eyebrows. "I'm guessing you've been to one?"

"Oh yeah! I went a lot when I was a kid," he nods. "My parents used to take me and my brother to Disney World every year," he says as he makes a left off my street and towards the highway. "When we'd go, my mom would always make sure we'd have time to go to the beach at least once. She always wanted to go to Miami, but my dad hated driving the extra hours, so she settled for the one in Orlando. It's not nearly as pretty as the beaches further south though," he pauses. "Now that I think about it, the last time I went to the beach was when I was ten years old, so wow... that was ten years ago," he chuckles.

"That sounds so fun. I've never been to Disney either. I've lived here in Forest my whole life. I've never even left Illinois. I guess I've been sheltered," I shrug with a slight giggle. *I hope I just didn't make myself sound boring.*

Max laughs at my comment which alleviates my nerves, so I guess I didn't sound as boring as I thought.

About forty minutes later, we arrive at Avery's which is right off the highway when you take the first exit into Townshed. I was slightly internally panicking the whole way here, but I think I held a good poker face because Max didn't seem to notice. If he did, well then, he didn't say anything. My accident didn't happen on the highway, but all the fast cars and lights made me nervous. I'm guessing I felt that way because that was the first time that I was in so much traffic since my accident happened. There was a small worry in the back of my head that we were going to crash but that was just my anxiety talking and I'm trying to keep reminding myself that.

Max and I are sitting across from each other by the water at Avery's. A railing decorated with warm string lights, divides the dark lake and our small two-person seater table. The tranquility of the lake water is perfect even though it's almost pitch black, and the décor of Avery's is definitely tropical, like Max said it would be. The exterior of the building's wall is decorated with different beach photos, while warm lights string the fake plastic palm trees that are placed throughout the patio. Our waiter just dropped off my shrimp alfredo pasta and Max's steak dinner only a few minutes ago.

"So, I noticed that you are no longer terminator," Max grins and I realize that he is talking about my arm.

"Oh, I actually got my cast off this morning. Finally, after having it on for five weeks," I sigh.

"Five weeks? Wow, what bloodshed happened upon the other person?" he teases.

I laugh at his comment while I try not to let alfredo sauce fall out of my mouth. "No bloodshed over here," I shake my head. "I got into a car accident a little while ago when I was driving to my best friend's apartment. So… what did you enroll in school for?" I go to change the subject because I don't want to tell him that I also went into a coma. I just don't want to go into details about the accident yet because I think it's too soon. We just started our date, so I shouldn't bring it down with my trauma this early. Besides, it's not really a first date worthy topic and I don't like talking about it anyway since it normally just frustrates me when I do.

"I enrolled in the music program. I write songs but I don't think they're that good," Max chuckles. "I really just want to learn as much as I can about the music industry.

I plan to go to Forest for two years and then transfer to another school to complete my bachelors, but I don't know which college I'll transfer to yet," he answers before taking a bite of his steak.

"I've never met anyone that writes songs. Does that mean you sing too?" I ask as I twirl my pasta on my plate before I take a bite.

"Only to my brother," he smirks as he looks side to side in an embarrassing gesture and it makes me bust out laughing. "He's my roommate," Max continues. "He's the only one that really ever hears me when I'm making music. No one else has ever heard me sing besides him."

"Oh, okay," I giggle as I finish wiping my mouth with a cloth napkin. "That makes sense."

"So, what about you? What did you enroll for?" he asks.

"I enrolled for my degree in teaching. I think I want to be a language arts teacher," I answer.

"What grade do you want to teach?"

"I don't really have a specific grade in mind, but I know that I want to teach Middle school. I just can't wait to finally start college since I had to-" I pause as I realize that I am almost about to tell him that I was in a coma. Instead, I say, "-wait for my boss to approve cutting my hours down at work. I'm going to have to drop from full time to part time when I start classes; that way, I can have enough time for school."

I'm technically not entirely lying because I will have to cut my hours at work when I do start classes in a few weeks, but I didn't have to wait for my boss to approve that before enrolling.

"Yeah, I can't wait to start college too," Max agrees, as he seemingly doesn't notice my white lie. "The quicker I get a degree, the quicker I'll be able to leave Stoney's."

"Oh, didn't you say that you just started working there?" I innocently ask.

"Yeah, I mean, don't get me wrong," he says, "It's not like I hate the job but honestly, I don't enjoy working there that much. My managers cool and my coworkers seem fine so far but working there has made me more excited to start school. I've never worked customer service until now and it's not fun," he laughs.

"Yeah, customer service sucks," I agree. "I'm a receptionist at a salon so believe me I understand. I'm sure you have to deal with more annoying customers since you're handling their food but the customers at the salon that I deal with can get pretty rude sometimes. I've been working there for two years, but I only got the job out of luck. It was the first place I went to when I turned seventeen, and they interviewed me right there. I got hired right on the spot."

"That is lucky. It was a struggle for me to find my first job. I tried getting a job everywhere in this town, but no one wanted a skinny seventeen-year-old like me around here," he laughs.

"Oh, you grew up here in Townshed?"

Max nods. "Yeah. I moved out to Forest Hill a year ago with my brother."

No wonder Max seems different. He's not a city boy. None of the guys that I went to high school with are as respectable and chill as he is.

"I can't picture you as a skinny seventeen-year-old," I grin before I take a bite of my pasta.

"I was," he sighs with a half smirk. "And I'm not proud of it."

Twenty minutes later, we finished our dinner and then Max drove me home. I couldn't have expected anything more from a first date. He has truly been the definition of a gentleman the whole time, even up until now as he walks me through the entrance of my apartment building and all the way down the first-floor hallway to my door which is the twelfth apartment on the left.

"I had a really good time tonight," he says as we approach my front door.

"Me too," I gulp. I have my back toward my door and I'm holding my purse by the strap tightly.

I don't remember feeling this way with Nate. Ever.

Max takes a step closer to me to reach for my hands, so I release my grip from my purse to reach his. I look down at our interlocked fingers. His hands nearly swallow mine since they are twice the size. I didn't think about what would happen during this moment. My heart is pounding so badly that I feel like it's audible to the hallway.

I hope he can't tell how nervous I am.

Moving my gaze from our hands up to Max's eyes, I catch a glimpse of his lips coming down toward me and I reach up to meet them with mine. After a few seconds, we let go.

Brushing the tip of his nose down mine, he says, "have a good night, Jen."

"You too," I manage to get the words out before releasing his hands. I fumble to look for my keys in my purse to unlock my door.

When I get in my apartment, I feel my heart still racing but the nervous sensation that I was feeling in the hallway is gone. I didn't even realize that I was smiling until I just caught my reflection through the mirror in the hall of my doorway.

CHAPTER 5

I was way too restless throughout the whole night after my date with Max because I was on a bit of a high from how happy I was feeling. However, then somewhere along the night my brain shifted into thinking about my accident, and that happiness quickly faded. I didn't fall asleep until about two in the morning and I woke up at 9:00 a.m. when my alarm went off. I quickly showered and then left my apartment to drive straight to Burr Oak Road. If the police aren't going to help me, then it's time that I figure out who this person is on my own.

This is my first time driving back on Burr Oak since my accident happened. I would only take this route to get to Michelle's apartment since it's the shortest and easiest way to get there. There are three other ways to get to her apartment from mine, but I usually take this one, ironically to avoid traffic as the other two routes are more populated since they are main roads.

As I am approaching just about five hundred feet before the curve of where the accident happened, I slow my shaky beamer down so I can pull it off the side of the road and into the grass. I park it so far into the grass, that my passenger door brushes up against the tree branches. I get out and lean against my door. There are no cars or people around me right now. The only sign on the road is a curved right black arrow which is placed just fifty feet before where the road starts to bend.

Standing here in near silence makes me think back to the image that I saw of my car after I got out of my coma. Even though, I can't recall the accident fully happening, I do know that my car spun out of control so badly that it ended up landing in the woods. It was *completely* totaled. My front windshield was smashed to pieces and my tires were all torn apart. I could only imagine how loud the accident was, especially since it happened at night.

I've never been in a car accident before that day, and I've only ever seen one happen in real life one time. I saw someone get rear ended at a red light across the road at an intersection. It was a minor crash but now that I think about it, I still heard it happen from across the busy street. *I wonder if my accident was loud enough for someone from one of the houses further down the road to hear it.* Officer Rodriguez told me that they questioned residents in the area, but she said no one saw a thing.

Would it be too invasive to knock on the nearest door and ask myself?

I guess I won't know until I try. This is what I came here to do; to look for clues. I already summoned up enough courage to drive back on this road so I might as well keep going.

I get back in my car and close my door. "I can do this," I exhale. "I can get past this," I say, trying to give myself a pep talk out loud.

I inhale and exhale a good number of times before putting my car key in the ignition, turning the engine on, and then shifting the gear into drive. Slowly, *very slowly,* I press my right foot on to the gas pedal and apply pressure to drive back on to the street.

When I do, I see a black four door car suddenly driving

up behind me in my rear-view mirror. *What perfect timing.*

I try to speed up some more since I know I am going *way* under the speed limit but as I get closer to the curve, my body starts shaking and it makes me ease my foot off the gas. I can't keep my foot steady anymore. I feel a panic attack coming on and it is *not the time for it.*

The car behind me is now approaching faster, just like the thud of my heartbeat. I want to wave at the driver to go around me, but I am way too close to the curve now. If they drive around me, the car will have to go into the other lane which could cause an accident if someone is coming from the other way.

The driver is right on my bumper now. If I were to slam on my breaks, they will probably rear-end me, so I press my foot on to the gas pedal harder, bringing the speed up. The curve is a quick ninety-degree bend. *I can make it around in less than ten seconds, I know it.* While I inhale deep and keep my eyes straight ahead, I begin to drive around it.

My heart is racing, but I somehow make it around the curve only seconds later. I'm pulling my car off on to the side of the road now, so the impatient asshole in the car behind me can go around and I can give myself a moment to calm down. The car's tires squeal when they dramatically floor pass me on the road, and I hear them shout some profanity at me through their open windows just as I get my car off the road.

My heart is still racing but at the same time I feel a sense of accomplishment. I take a moment to let what I just accomplished sink in, and a sudden rush of adrenaline runs through me. *I need to keep going.*

I head straight until I see less of the trees and the

neighborhood begins.

The first house that I come upon is about two hundred feet down and is on the left side of the road. It's a small single-family home with a large front yard and narrow driveway. I pull in and park my car at the very end of it.

Walking up to the door, I try to remind myself to keep calm. I'm not that much of a confrontational person if I don't have to be, but I know my mind won't rest until I do this myself. After I knock twice, I take a step back and wait a few seconds.

"Can I help you?" An elderly man who looks to be in at least his late seventies answers the door.

"Hi. Uh," I hesitate as I realize I have not thoroughly thought about what I am going to say.

"Can I help you, young lady?" he repeats. *His voice sounds agitated already.*

"Sorry... uh, yes. I'm hoping you can, sir. My name is Jen," I try to say confidently.

"Your name is what? Speak up. I can't hear you," he says in a hastier voice.

I clear my throat before I go to speak louder. "I said, my name is JEN. I am sorry to bother you, but I was wondering if you could answer a quick question for me. I-"

"No soliciting here. I got no answers for you," he interrupts me and goes to shut the door, but I put my palm against it so he can't close it.

"W-wait," I stutter. "I'm not soliciting. I was just wondering if you remember hearing a car crash about a few weeks ago. It happened on Saturday September 20th after 11-"

"I don't remember what I ate yesterday, dear. Sorry can't help you." He goes to close his door again, but I stop him.

"Okay, well, wait. Hold on! Did the cops ever come by here to ask you about a hit and run recently?" I desperately ask with my hand still pressed against the door.

"Nope. No cops came around here. Can't help you," he says again. "Now remove your hand."

I get back in my car and instead of reversing out of his driveway and going back in the direction that I came from; I continue to drive into the neighborhood toward the four way stop sign. The stop sign is about a mile down and it's normally where I take a right to get to Michelle's apartment. Between this guy's house and the stop sign, there are only four more houses on this street, so I decide to stop at each one.

I get to the next house and ring the doorbell three times, but no one answers so I head to the third, then to the fourth house on the block. Just like the grouchy old man, the people who lived at the third and fourth houses did not help me, although they were nicer to me. Both residents told me that they did not hear anything, and the cops never came by to question them. I just knocked on the door of the last house before the stop sign, hoping that I'll get a different answer from all the previous neighbors this time.

"Hello?" a woman wearing a nurse's uniform who looks to be in her mid-thirties, answers the door.

"Hi. Uh, I'm sorry to bother you. My name is Jen. I just have a quick question," I begin. "So, I was in a car accident a few weeks ago on September 20th. Someone crashed into me and drove away. The driver hasn't been caught by the police yet and I'm just here because I was wondering if you might've possibly heard or seen anything around

EVERYTHING LED ME TO YOU

that time?"

The woman looks at me with a puzzled face which seems like my answer is a no. "I know. This is totally random. Sorry to bother you," I shake my head and go to turn away. *I'm just wasting my time and probably hers too.* "I'm just going to go-"

"No, no, wait," she says, stopping me. "I did see something a few weeks ago but I don't remember what the date was exactly. I saw a truck speeding past here one night when I was getting in my car to leave for my night shift. I remember because it had a the left headlight was out and it was swerving a bit, then it flew through the stop sign," she pauses as she shakes her head, "but I told the police that already. I called them on my way to work that night."

"You did?" I gasp. "You don't remember what day at all?"

She shakes her head as she scrunches her mouth, "No I don't know the date, but I know it was a Saturday or Sunday night because I only work weekends."

"Do you remember what it looked like or what kind of truck it was? What did the cops say when you told them?" I gasp again. I can't get my questions out fast enough.

"Oh, I'm not sure what kind of truck it was," she pauses to think about it, "It was a pickup truck, I know that. I think the color of it was maybe... blue or black, but I honestly am not one hundred percent sure about that. It was too dark out," she tells me as she scrunches her forehead.

She looks just as confused as I feel. Officer Rodriguez asked me if the headlights looked like they were on a truck when I woke up, but I never thought twice about it. Now it makes sense why she asked me. I just thought that she was doing her job in trying to narrow the type of vehicle that hit me. Now, I'm not so sure of that anymore.

"What did the cops say when you told them this?" I ask.

"They just took my statement on the phone and that was it. I never heard anything since. I'm sorry, I really wish I could help you more," she says kindly. "But I am glad you're okay, now."

I give her a half smile. *I wish the officers had the same tone as her.*

"Thanks. Well, I'll let you go. Thank you for your help again," I say, then I get back in my car.

Officer Rodriguez asked me if the headlights were on a higher vehicle, like a truck... I didn't think anything of it at the time, but after hearing what that nurse just told me, this seems like too much of a coincidence. She didn't remember the exact day that she saw the truck, but she said it was Saturday or Sunday... and my accident was on a Saturday night. *But if the truck that she saw was the vehicle that hit me, then why would it be driving this way?*

They hit me head on, so they were coming from this direction. Why would it drive back the way it came from? I would think that the person would just continue driving in the direction they were originally going. *I need to find out more about this truck just for my own peace of mind. Something isn't right... I feel it.*

I desperately want to go to the police station right now and raise hell, but I am beginning to get a headache, and I know I should take the medicine that my doctor prescribed me. Thankfully, I haven't had a lot of headaches since I got out of my coma but when I do get them, they come quickly, and I know I need to get my medication right away. I'm not used to having pills on me except my birth control because I've never needed any other medication before this, and I keep leaving it at home. Of course, whenever I need it, I barely have it on me.

While I drive home, I'll just call Officer Rodriguez instead of going into the police station. She's the one who questioned me about a truck originally, so she should have the answers for me.

"Forest Hill Police," a male officer answers the phone a few seconds after I call.

"Hello. Is Officer Rodriguez there?" I ask.

"No, she left an hour ago. Can I take a message?" he responds. I wait a moment to think about leaving one before I decide that it will probably do no good. I need to talk to Officer Rodriguez in person again. I'm going to make her give me a reason to why she didn't tell me that the neighbor reported the truck.

"Uh, no, no. It's fine. Thanks," I say and end the call. I'll just wait to stop at the station to speak with her in the morning before I go to work tomorrow. My shift doesn't start until noon, so I'll wake up early. That way, I can be at the station by 8:00 a.m. and hopefully, Officer Rodriguez will be there.

CHAPTER 6

It was somewhere around three in the morning when I finally fell asleep because once again my mind was too restless. I ended up sleeping two hours past my 7:00 a.m. alarm and I immediately showered, got myself ready for work and then drove straight to the police station. I just walked in the lobby and am standing in front of an officer who is sitting behind the front desk.

"Excuse me? I need to speak to Officer Rodriguez," I say as I make sure to make my voice sound as assertive as I can.

"She was just here a few minutes ago but she had to leave for something. Can I leave a message for her?"

"Uh, no," I sigh. "When will she be back?"

"I'm not sure. Is there something I can help you with though?" The officer's tone is surprisingly friendlier than Officer Rodriguez is. *I really want to talk to officer Rodriguez, but I can't sit here and wait for her. It's already 11:00 a.m. and I do have to get to work in an hour...*

"Well, I guess it might not matter who I really talk to," I pause. "I just have a question about my case. It's number 6875. Can you please look it up?"

After a few seconds of typing onto her keyboard, the officer exchanges her eyesight from the computer and looks at me with a puzzled face. "Your case is closed. Weren't you notified?"

Through gritted teeth I say, "yes, I was notified but I have a question about it. I wasn't told anything about a truck. Why didn't anyone tell me what the neighbor saw?"

The cop tilts her head slightly. "I'm sorry, what are you talking about?"

"Why didn't anyone tell me that one of the neighbors reported a suspicious truck?" I demand. "Isn't that in the report? I've been told by Officer Rodriguez that there were no leads but uh, that sounds like a lead to me." I can hear the anger grow in my voice as I speak. I don't want to take it out on this lady but it's difficult to control.

"Oh, let me see. Hold on," she tells me while she scrolls through the report.

As I wait, I realize that I am standing with my hands on my hips, and I am tapping my right foot wildly against the floor. I know I need to control my aggravation right now but it's becoming increasingly difficult to.

"It does say that someone made a report of a suspicious vehicle the night of your accident," she confirms, and my eyebrows raise in excitement.

"But it says that it was ruled out after you made a statement where you reported that you did not think that the vehicle was it when Officer Rodriguez asked you about it."

I blink a few times and I shake my head. "No, no, no. That is not what happened," I insist. "I was ASKED IF I THOUGHT the headlights that I saw were higher than my car, like as if they could have been on a truck, and I answered that I WASN'T SURE if they were or not. I did not say to rule out the truck. She didn't even tell me that someone reported it!"

"I'm very sor-"

"All I ever hear is I'm sorry from you people," I cut her words off.

"I wish I could help you more," the officer says in a kind tone so I don't take it out on her. There is no point in arguing with her. She's not even the one on my case. She's only reading what's on her computer screen anyway. I have to wait and talk to Officer Rodriguez. I'll just have to deal with this tomorrow.

"Yeah, that makes two of us," I mumble and turn to walk out of the lobby. As I am marching out of the police station, my phone buzzes in my back jean pocket and I check it to see that it's a text message from Max.

It reads - **Hi, Jen. I had a great time with you. I was wondering if you'd like to go out with me again this Friday. There is a new lounge near Millennium Park in the city, and I'd like to take you. They have live bands on Friday nights.**

As I read the text, my mood is instantly lifted. My doctor told me to stay away from loud noises for a while but if the band is playing in a lounge, then I don't think the music should be too loud for me.

I text him back - **Yes, I'd love too,** with a smiley emoticon.

Seconds later, he replies - **Great! I'll pick you up at 8:00 p.m. Do you mind if we take the train? I don't want to waste time looking for parking.**

Hell no, I wouldn't mind! I haven't been back on the highway since our first date, and I don't want a repeat of another internal panic attack. It will take at least an hour and a half to get downtown if we drive and there will be twice as much traffic around that time anyway. The train will only take about forty-five minutes. I text him back that I don't mind at all, and he confirms our date before I pull out of the parking lot and drive to work.

—

I only slept for about three or four hours again last night. My mind was so consumed with what the neighbor told me; I could barely sleep. I set an alarm for 7:00 a.m. again so I could get up early enough to catch Officer Rodriguez and this time I woke up for it. After spending ten minutes in the police station's lobby, I finally see her start walking toward me. She is looking at me like she doesn't remember who I am.

"Hello, ma'am. I am Officer Rodriguez. Can I help you?" she asks as she approaches me.

"You don't remember me?" I tilt my head to the side and scrunch my forehead. "My name is Jennifer Russo. I was in a car accident a few weeks ago. I was in a coma. You just spoke to me on the phone the other day."

She looks at me for a second with confusion before I see the realization start to come upon her face. "Oh, yes. I remember you. I believe you called me and my coworkers here, garbage."

Shit… I forgot I said that.

"Uh, yeah sorry about that," I embarrassingly say. "I've been a little aggravated lately. You know, giving my situation and all." I press my lips together.

Officer Rodriguez gives me a forced smile. "Follow me," she says as she leads me out of the lobby and back to her desk.

"So, Jennifer, what can I help you with today?" She asks as she sits down in her chair while I sit in the one across from her.

"I have some questions about my case," I answer.

Officer Rodriguez presses her lips into a half-smile and

shakes her head. "I'm sorry but I told you that your case is already closed. There is just nothing I can do anymore. I don't have any leads. I-"

"Yes, you do have a lead!" I interrupt her. "That's why I'm here. I spoke to a resident that lives about a mile down from where my accident happened, and she told me that she saw a suspicious truck drive by her house around that time. She said it was speeding past her house and one of the headlights were out. Why didn't you tell me that when you asked me about a truck in the hospital? Did you investigate that tip at all?"

"Yes," she nods her head. "I did investigate that tip. That's why I asked you if the headlights looked like they might have been on a truck, but you told me that they weren't, dear."

"Uh, no. That's not what I said. I said I *didn't remember* if the headlights were on a truck or not."

"I don't want to be rude, but you did just wake up from a coma, Jennifer. You may not be remembering our conversation word for word."

Officer Rodriguez rests her forearms on the desk. She is starting to give me a condescending look and it's beginning to irritate me even more.

"Are you fucking kidding me right now?" I scoff. The words just left my mouth unintentionally, but I have no regret.

"Ma'am, watch your language when you are speaking to the police," Officer Rodriguez says in a sterner voice, but her tone doesn't intimidate me. It just infuriates me more.

"Don't tell me to watch my language. I'm not a child. I'm trying to get you to do your job here! I'm aggravated! I have a right to be."

Is she serious right now? I have an urge to leap over the desk and punch that look off her face, but I won't.

"I understand your frustration Jennifer, but I can't do anything more. Unless you can give me an actual description of the truck or a license plate to run, then I still have no leads," she pauses. "Plus, the statement from the witness doesn't quite match anyway. The vehicle hit you head on which means that the person that was driving it likely would have continued driving in the same direction they were originally heading. I don't believe they would have turned around."

"Okay, but what if they did though?" I cross my arms against my torso.

"Listen, I know you've been through a lot, but you can't go off investigating on your own, Jennifer. That's our job," Officer Rodriguez gives me a hard look. "I would suggest not going back to the neighborhood and harassing the neighbors for your own safety. I think the best thing you need to do is get past everything. May I suggest talking to someone about your trauma? Maybe you can speak to a psychologist?"

A psychologist? That's her solution? I remain here in my chair and stare at her with straight confusion on my face. My eyes feel like they are about to pop out of my head right now.

"No, no, no. I can't get past this," I say in a louder tone as I stand up from my chair. "You said that you didn't have a description of the vehicle, but you did! The damn neighbor gave it to you."

"It wasn't a good enough description, Jennifer. I'd need more details other than just a missing headlight. It's a very vague description. Why don't you sit and calm down right now? Your hands are turning red."

She gestures down to my hands that are tightly gripped on to the back of the chair, but I don't sit down and continue standing. *I can't sit down. I'm livid at the moment.* She's completely dismissing me, and I'm appalled by it.

"Don't you want this person to get caught? What if they did this to me on purpose? What if they've done it before or they'll do it again?" I shout. "I almost died! You realize that right?"

"Ma'am, please lower your voice," Officer Rodriguez says as she stands up from behind her desk.

"No! I'm done just waiting around!" I am still standing but I let go of the chair and now I'm clenching my fists at my sides. *I can't calm down.* This woman is seriously looking me in the eyes and telling me that I don't recall our conversation, but I remember every damn word from it.

"Please, sit down. If you don't calm down, I will have to detain you."

"Detain me for what? Asking about my case?" My voice is louder and filled with more fury. I've never felt so aggravated in my life before. I didn't even feel this angry when I found out that Nate cheated on me.

Suddenly, I feel hands on my wrists, and I look to my left to see that it's another officer holding them. "Please relax," he says but at this point I can't relax, especially since he's squeezing my wrists like this.

"Let go of me!" Out of instinct, I'm starting to struggle but the more I do, the tighter he holds onto me. *This is reminding me of the white room, and I don't like it.* "You're seriously arresting me right now? For what?" I gasp as I look at Officer Rodriguez.

"Because I don't think you are mentally stable right now. You will be detained until you can calm down," she says as I feel handcuffs getting clasped around my wrists by the male officer. "I think you just need to calm down. If you keep fighting, you will be charged for resisting of arrest. Please, Jennifer. I am just trying to get you to relax."

"Resisting arrest?!" I gasp.

Now she thinks that I'm mentally unstable? Seriously? If anything, this whole situation is what is making me mentally unstable.

I know that I should calm myself down before I make things worse... but then again, how much worse can things get? I'm already being led away from the desk in handcuffs. The next thing I know, I am sitting in an empty cell by myself.

CHAPTER 7

Officer Rodriguez released me from the police station after keeping me detained for four hours yesterday. Once I got put in the cell, I calmed down when I realized that my emotions were not making anything better. I was asked if I wanted to call anyone to come get me while I was there, but I was too stubborn and said no. The only people I would have called are either my parents or Michelle and I don't need any of them to worry about me anymore, so I toughened it out and waited for Officer Rodriguez to deem me *stable again*.

All officer Rodriguez wanted from me was to calm down so that is what I did. Although, I'll admit that it was hard to keep from crying in the cell because I was so frustrated with myself, but I'm glad I contained my composure. When Officer Rodriguez did release me, she made sure to warn me again of the dangers of investigating on my own which I politely nodded and nearly ran out of the station.

When I turned on my phone once I got home, I had one missed call from Michelle, and then another missed call and two text messages from my mom. I called them back right away and lied to the both of them that I was sleeping. I didn't answer my phone in four hours, and they already started to worry. I could only imagine what they would have done if they got a call from the police station.

I woke up a half hour ago and just made some eggs for breakfast. After I eat, I am going to go for a light jog to clear my mind from everything. My doctor told me I can exercise but I need to be careful when I do. I can run as long as it's not a crazy marathon which I never plan to take part of ever. I can barely run two hundred feet without having to stop to catch my breath anyway, but I like to jog to just clear my mind. I started jogging when I was dealing with my breakup with Nate, and I have not gone for one since I awoke out of the coma. After getting put in a jail cell yesterday, I definitely need to go for a jog and clear my mind. I never imagined getting in trouble with the police but then again, I never imagined dying for a week either.

Before I go outside, I decide to check my mail from the pile that I picked up on Saturday. In it, is an envelope from the hospital and when I pick it up, I get a tight feeling in my chest. I was told by the nurse who ran my insurance that I should be covered but I never fully believed her. As I open the envelope, my suspicions are confirmed when I see the amount of two thousand dollars next to the words *amount due* in the top right-hand corner of the paper. I skim over three pointless paragraphs that explain absolutely no reason for why I'm being charged until I see that the total is due in three months.

First, it's my car insurance. Now it's my health insurance. At least I was accustomed to paying my monthly car payment before the accident, so that's not really an added bill... but this hospital bill is. I just used basically all my savings to pay for the first quarter of school too. I swear that every day since I've awoken from my coma, life just wants to keep testing me. I've only had a few panic attacks before the accident happened but now, I feel one coming on for a third time this month.

I don't like it and I'm not going to let it take over me. I'm not going to let the other driver keep control of my life. I already feel like a different person than I was before the accident and it's not fair that the person responsible for that is still out there. I have the rest of the day off so I might as well make use of it. Instead of going for a jog, I am going back to Burr Oak Road. I'm working the afternoon shift today, so I don't go into work until 2:00 p.m. which means I have a few hours to drive around the city and search for this mysterious truck.

Ten minutes later, I find myself driving on Burr Oak Road. I just drove around the curve of where my accident happened, and I had way more confidence than I did when the other day when I first drove through. I already passed the house of where the old man lives that I spoke to and now, I am pulling into the driveway of the second house on the block. Since no one answered the first time, I figure that I should try again.

After two knocks, a young woman who looks just a couple years older than me, opens the door while holding a baby on her right side. "Can I help you?" she asks.

"Hi, my name is Jen. I'm so sorry to bother you. I knocked on your door the other day, but no one was home. This might sound weird," I pause, "but I was in a car accident on September 20th... The person drove off and I am trying to figure out who they are, so I was just wondering if you might've saw or heard anything odd around that time. It was after 11:00 p.m."

The woman shakes her head. "Oh no, I don't recall hearing anything. I was probably sleeping by then. Let me ask my boyfriend."

She calls to him, but I hear him respond that he didn't hear or see anything either. "I'm sorry we can't help you," she says when she directs her attention back to me, so I thank her and then get back into my car to keep driving down Burr.

As I was passing by the third house, I spotted a camera above the lady's garage door, so I quickly turned my car around and parked into her driveway. I didn't notice the camera when I stopped at her house the other day. If I did, I would have asked her about it. After a few knocks, she opens the door. "Hi, sorry to bother you again," I say.

"Oh, uh, hello," she pauses. "I already told you that I didn't see anything."

"Right, but maybe your camera might've?" I suggest as I point over to the garage.

She follows my finger with her eyes. "Oh, I forgot about that. My husband put it up last year after our garage got broken into. I honestly don't know if it even works. I'll have to ask him about it but he's not here right now. He's at work."

"Oh, that's okay. Can I leave you my number and you can just text me if you see anything? I'm just looking to see if a dark colored pickup truck with a missing left headlight passed by. I'm so-so sorry to bother you with this," I tell her because I really am. I don't like being an inconvenience or an annoyance and that's all I have felt like I've been to everyone lately.

She agrees to contact me, so I give her my number and name to put in her cellphone. Then I thank her again and get back in my car to continue my search.

As I drive by the nurse's house and I approach the stop sign, I remember that's she told me, she saw the truck speed right through it, so I decide to drive straight in the same direction. If the truck went this way, then someone else had to see something too. Maybe there is another house on the block with a security camera too.

Once I pass through the stop sign, I drive about an eighth of a mile down until I see a gas station on the left side of the road. I've gone in there only a handful of times. I pull into the parking lot, and I notice that there are two cameras mounted outside of the entrance doors.

When I go into the store, a teenage boy is sitting behind the counter. There is a large TV monitor right next to him with a grid of camera angles that show both the interior and exterior of the store and parking lot, so I walk over to the counter to look closer at the screen. I can only see a portion of the road near the entrance and exit of the parking lot. If the truck continued driving down this street like the nurse said, then surely this camera would have caught it because the person would have had to pass by.

"Excuse me, is your manager here?" I ask the cashier.

He looks up from his cell phone without answering me, then gets off his chair and walks out from behind the counter and into a side door off to the right, that says employees only. A minute or so later, a woman about two inches taller than me and maybe in her late twenties walks out from the door.

"Hello. Can I help you?" She tilts her head a bit and crosses her arms at her torso. She doesn't have a friendly face.

"Uh, Hello. My name is Jen. I'm sorry to bother you but I was wondering if you could possibly help me. I was the victim of a hit and run a few weeks ago and I am trying to remember details about my accident. I think the driver was heading this way and I noticed that you have a security camera in the front entrance... I was wondering if you could maybe show me the footage from September 20th, that is," I pause, "if you have it still?"

The woman has a ponderous look on her face as she scrunches her forehead. I hear her start to make the *hmm* sound with her lips which means she is probably about to say no, so I decide to try and get dramatic. I look over at the cameras and sigh loudly before I clear my throat. "Listen, I almost died that night. I went into a coma for a week and I just want to find out who crashed into me. The cops aren't helping me, so I'm off investigating on my own. I really think I know what the truck looks like, but I don't know what the plate number is so I was hoping your cameras might have caught it. Please, can you at least check to see if you still have the footage? I know this sounds crazy. I just can't get past what happened to me... it's been really hard."

After a few seconds of pondering my questions, she says, "follow me."

"REALLY?" I gasp in surprise before I follow her through the door to her small office.

She sits down behind her desk and asks, "what time again?"

"Sometime around 11:00 p.m."

A moment passes before she gestures for me to walk behind the desk so I can see the screen with her. As she holds the mouse down on the forward button to scan through the black and white footage quicker, my heart nearly stops when I catch a quick glance of the tailgate of a truck go by. "Stop!" I gasp.

She stops the video and plays it back a few frames. Then she plays it in real time and pauses it just as the back end of the vehicle is leaving the screen. It's a dark pickup truck but it doesn't look like it was speeding, and both headlights work.

"Hmm, I don't think that's it. Keep going, please," I say, and she continues to play the footage.

We both watch the video play out in fast forward for a few more minutes where we see two more cars pass by. It isn't until around 11:23 p.m. when we see a new truck drive by, and she stops the footage, then plays it back. The truck is definitely speeding, and the left headlight is out. I can't tell what the color of the truck is since the footage is black and white because it's nighttime, but the color of it does look like it is dark.

"I-- I think that's it," I surprisingly say as I stare at the screen.

She pauses the video on the tail gate of the truck. The license plate can't be seen clearly but I can tell by the tree shape on the right side of the plate that it is a Forest Hill plate. All plates registered in Forest Hill have a tree on it, no matter the style of the plate. So, now I know that the driver lives here… I just wish I could make out the letters and numbers clearly.

"You can't give me this footage, can you?" I ask with a cynical face.

She shakes her head. "No, but you can take a picture or video of it with your phone, if you want."

"Really?" I gasp in excitement as I pull my phone out of my purse. I didn't expect that she'd be so nice about this. "This is really helpful. Thank you so much."

"I've had experience with cops not helping," she says in a low tone. "I didn't go through an accident or anything like you described but I think I know what you're going through with the police not helping. They can be very," she pauses, "hard to deal with."

Finally, someone who understands me.

"Just don't have them come looking for this footage here. I'm deleting it once you leave. I'm sorry but I don't want them coming around here if I don't need to be involved."

"Oh, don't worry. I won't tell them a thing," I say. "I don't really plan on dealing with them again anyways." I record a few seconds of the video with my cell phone. Then I thank her again before going back to my car to continue driving down Burr.

I'm not really surprised at what that manager told me, not after what I've experienced with the police. I didn't want to ask her about her own experience with them because I'm sure whatever it is probably wasn't very pleasant. It sure as hell hasn't been for me.

I got to the nearest house after the gas station, and I knocked three times, but no one answered. The next house didn't have any cameras either and the woman who answered was a babysitter. She wasn't even at their house the night of my accident. When I came up to the next house, I immediately spot a camera mounted by the front door, so I pulled into the driveway.

A man, maybe around fifty years old or so, answers a few seconds after I ring the doorbell. I tell him my story and thankfully, he doesn't mind checking his camera for me. He even invites me inside of his house to look with him. I have never walked into a stranger's house, let alone one of an older man that I've never met... and every movie that I have watched with a naïve character that ends up kidnapped, raped, murdered... or all three, is beginning to run through my head.

However, against my better judgement and nerves, I still walk into his home. I keep my keys firmly in my hand, letting my paranoia take over. It may be my anxiety talking but I still hold onto them just in case I need to defend myself.

Just as I step into the doorway, my mind is set at ease when I see two children run from down the stairs, so I relax my grip. *I need to stop being so paranoid.* The guy leads me to his office which is straight down the hallway through his living room. He sits behind his desk and asks me for the date again.

"It would be on September 20th, around the time of 11:23 p.m.," I answer.

After scrubbing through two minutes of the footage and seeing only two cars pass by, he stops it around the time of 11:25 p.m. when a truck appears on screen. My pulse quickens when I realize that it's the same one that sped by the convenience store. "Right there! That's it! Can you zoom in, please?"

He zooms in on the truck, but it doesn't help. The license plate is clearer on his camera rather than what the camera caught at the convenience store, but I still can't make out the letters or numbers on the license plate. I think the first letter is a *T*, but I have no idea what the rest are.

"Oh, I think this might be it! Do you mind if I record a video with my cell phone?" I ask.

He nods for me to go ahead, and I record a few seconds of it with my phone when he replays the video for me. I thank him one more time before I leave and get back in my car.

When I go to back out of his driveway, I think about how the pickup was still driving this way and where it could have gone next. There is a stop light about three hundred feet ahead and they could have only gone either left or right at it. If they went right, they would have driven past the grocery store which is a half mile down. If they turned left at the light, they would have passed the outdoor strip mall which is only about half a mile down in the opposite direction.

Either way, both the grocery store and strip malls must have security cameras. I'll just have to ask the managers to see the footage, like I asked the manager at the gas station. I have about two hours until my shift starts at work, and I still have to go home and get ready, but I can't quit my search now. I shamelessly send a text message to my boss to let her know that I'll be coming in late today because I'm having car trouble. Then, I decide to take a right at the light.

When I got to the grocery store, I waited about ten minutes at customer service for the manager. Unfortunately, once he did finally come up to me, he didn't let me see any footage. He was pretty persistent on his answer, so I didn't put up much of a fight. After he rejected me, I drove back in the opposite direction toward the strip mall. I first stopped into the nail salon because there was a camera mounted right outside the entrance of it, but the person that I spoke to told me they didn't have access to it, only the building owner did. And no, of course, the person I spoke to didn't give me the owners number because they didn't have it.

When they told me that, I did not even try to go in any of the rest of the shops because if the people at the nail's salon didn't have the owner's number, then the rest of the five shops in the mall probably didn't either. So, I left and drove around the surrounding neighborhood after that.

I only found two houses near the strip mall that had cameras outside, so I knocked on their doors and I explained my sad story for what has been, way too many times in one day. The lady who answered the door at the first house said she didn't have the footage from the twentieth anymore and the guy at the other house told me that his cameras didn't even work.

When I got back in my car and looked at my phone as I was leaving his driveway, I realized that two hours had already passed by since I texted my boss. So, I finally stopped my investigation for the day and drove to work before giving my boss the decision to fire me.

CHAPTER 8

"I brought you this dress for tonight," Michelle says as she hands me a baby blue long-sleeved V-neck slip dress that reaches just above my knees. Then she pulls out a pair of strappy black one-inch heels from the bag that she brought with her. "Here, these heels match perfectly."

I am getting ready for my second date with Max tonight, and she insisted on helping me this time. "Heels? You expect me to walk from the train and throughout the city in Heels? Heels aren't the best choice," I laugh.

"Maybe not for you." She shrugs as she gets up from my bed and goes into my closet to hand me my black knee high one-inch-tall, thick heeled boots. "I hate these boots, but they are the only other pair of shoes you have that will match that dress."

These boots aren't really the best for walking around a lot, but I'll take them over strappy skinny heels any day. I look at myself in my mirror after I put on the dress and boots. I can see Michelle sitting on my bed through the reflection smiling with approval. She is clearly satisfied with her outfit choice.

"What would you do without me?" She leaps up from the bed with her phone in hand. "I can't find Max on the gram yet."

"That's because you're not going to," I laugh. "I was right when I thought he didn't wasn't on social media. I asked him on the drive home last time. He said he doesn't like it. I don't know. He's... different from other guys. Maybe because he's a year older," I shrug. "I'm glad he doesn't have it. I think that's a good thing. I don't have to deal with the drama the internet brings. That's how Nate ended up cheating on me." I roll my eyes at the thought of it.

"Nate's in the past." Michelle leaps up from the bed. "You know, you've gotten really good at covering your scar." She notices it as she steps next to me and looks at our reflections through the mirror.

"I mean, two weeks has given me enough practice," I sigh.

"Speaking of accident, have you heard anything since you got all that footage?" she asks.

I already showed Michelle the videos I took at both the stores and the guy's house that I stopped at. I also told her that I went into the police station to talk to Officer Rodriguez, but I still didn't tell her that I went back a second time and got detained. I'm not in the mood for that conversation because I know it's just going to worry her so instead, I just shake my head, no.

"I can't believe they closed the case," she sighs. "I know you've been asked a dozen times, but you still can't remember anything about the vehicle yet?" She gives me a look of hope. "Does any part of the truck in that footage look rememberable at all?"

"I really wish." I roll my eyes. "You know how dark it is on Burr. The accident happened so quickly... I still can't believe it," I shake my head. "That nurse that I spoke to said she saw the truck passing by at night, on a weekend and her description matched perfectly to what I saw on the cameras... I don't know," I sigh. "It's just too much of a coincidence for me. I know it's a long shot, but my instincts aren't letting me let this go."

"Well, it does sound a little suspicious… but if that's them, then why would they be driving the opposite way? They hit you head on from that direction. Why would they turn around?" Michelle questions just as I and Officer Rodriguez had questioned too.

"I don't know," I shrug. "I thought about that too. I know that part doesn't really make sense but still… it's just all too much of a coincidence."

"I guess it is kind of weird that the cop asked you specifically if the headlights were on a truck," Michelle points out.

"Yeah, I realized that as soon as the nurse told me what she saw. I wish I realized it in the hospital though. By the way she phrased the question, it sounded like she was asking me if the lights were higher than my vehicle, like as if, she was trying to narrow down the type of vehicle or something," I shrug my shoulders and drop on the bed. "I just thought she was doing basic police work. I should have known. I should've asked more questions."

"It's not your fault. You had just got out of a coma, Jen. I'm surprised you were even aware enough to talk to her," Michelle says as she goes to my closet. She pulls out a small black shoulder strap purse and hands it to me. "Use this purse tonight. It matches your dress better than your other one."

I take it and go into my kitchen where my regular purse is sitting on the counter, so I can switch out my items into the cuter one she chose. Shortly after, we hear knocking on my door, and it makes us both look at each other instantly.

"Behave please," I tell her.

"I can never promise what comes out of my mouth," she responds with a proud smirk.

I open my front door to let Max into my apartment. He is wearing a plain dark blue button down long-sleeved collared shirt and dark denim jeans.

"Max, this is my best friend, Michelle. Michelle, meet Max," I say.

"Nice to meet you, Maxy," Michelle says as she looks him up and down. She squeezes his right bicep instead of shaking his hand and then smiles at me. "Muscular, good choice!"

Max softly laughs. It's more of an amusing laugh than anything. I don't think he was expecting that. "Nice to meet you, too."

"Well, you kids have fun tonight," she says as she grabs her purse and keys from my living room table. "Love you." She hugs me then turns to Max. "You hurt her, then I hurt you. Those muscles are no match for me," she smirks at him before heading out the door.

"I should've warned you," I grin at Max after she leaves.

"You didn't need to warn me. Her car was warning enough," he chuckles.

Michelle bought a blue four door Toyota Corolla a year ago and the first thing she did to it was plaster a two-foot-wide princess crown decal on her driver side door. Just recently, she added three bright purple star decals in the same size on top of her hood. I guess you could say her car matches her personality perfectly. Quite a few people around the city know her by it.

"That's Michelle for you," I laugh as we both walk out my door and head to his SUV.

—

70

Stepping off the train station and onto the busy Chicago streets in this dress with Max felt a little weird to me. Even though I can take the train into the city easily, I rarely ever do. The last time that I came downtown was around Christmas last year, when I went ice skating in Millennium Park, but I was with Michelle and some friends from high school. Nate wasn't even with us so that experience was way different than what I'm experiencing right now with Max. It's only a few minutes past 9:00 p.m. on a Friday night and the streets are busily packed with people already. These boots on my feet were a perfect choice because I'm sure I would have tripped or bumped into someone if I was wearing the skinnier heels.

Rollay's, the lounge that Max chose, is a bit of a hole in the wall cozy place. It is packed in between a sandwich shop and a restaurant a few blocks away from Millenium station, where we got off the train. The lounge is half the size of Stoney's, and it is vibrantly decorated with neon lights surrounding the bar and walls while the floors are decorated in a checkered pattern.

Our waiter just dropped off two gyro sandwiches and sodas at our table. We are sitting in the far back in a booth against the wall. There is a contemporary rock band called *Breakswitch* playing on the stage, and they sound fairly good.

"I just realized, I never even asked you if you like rock music," Max chuckles with a weary face before he takes a bite of his gyro.

"I wouldn't have said yes, if I didn't," I smile. "I don't normally choose rock as my first music choice, but I'm not opposed to it," I shrug. "I don't have a specific taste in music really. I like pretty much everything except for gospel, opera and heavy screamo."

"So, that means you like country too?" Max questions.

"Actually, yes. I do," I smirk while slightly squinting my eyes. "Why do you ask?"

"Because I barely ever meet anyone around our age that likes country," he laughs. "I grew up listening to it because of my parents so I was forced to like it. Rock and country are basically the only two music genres I listen to."

"Well, at least we have two genres that we like in common," I smile. "Speaking of music, what made you want to start studying it?" I ask before taking a sip of my drink.

"Well, I started writing songs when I turned sixteen, right after my parents died," he pauses as he slightly widens his eyes and draws his head back a bit. "Oh, sorry. I shouldn't have led with that."

"Oh, it's fine," I shrug as I look at him with concern. "Why would you apologize?"

"Most of the time when I start or end a sentence about my dead parents to anyone, they give me sad puppy eyes," he pauses as he smiles at me. "You're the first person that hasn't. Your face didn't even budge."

I admit that I am shocked of what Max just told me, but I guess I was good at not showing it. I've never met anyone so young with dead parents, but I don't think he should have to apologize when talking about them. I've never dealt with a death in my family, let alone parental death so I don't know what it's like, but I'm not scared of the conversation.

"You can tell me more... that is, if you'd like," I tell him as I keep a soft smile on my face.

His dark eyes dig deep into mine for a moment before he smiles back at me. "Well, they died five years ago in a car accident. Their car skidded across the highway when it was snowing" he pauses. "Anyway, after it happened, I guess I used rock music as, like, a coping mechanism because I was pretty angry for a while, but I'm not so much anymore. I've learned to cope with it now, but it still sucks," he pauses to shake his head as if he is trying to not bring the conversation down anymore. "Anyway, I ended up skipping a lot of school just to stay at home to learn my guitar and write songs, so I guess that's when I got into it. I'm actually surprised that I graduated because at one point, I stayed home for two weeks straight during my Senior year. I almost got kicked out if it weren't for my brother," he laughs. "He had to come down to the school and have a parent teacher meeting since he was my guardian at the time. It was extra hilarious because he had literally graduated only two years before that, and there he was, back in the principal's office acting as a parent."

"Oh my god, that had to be funny," I laugh in between bites of my gyro. "That was probably also really uncomfortable for him."

"Hell, yeah," he nods as I can tell he's reminiscing the moment by his smile. "The principal hated him when he was in school, even before our parents died. He was always a problem; never listened, got terrible grades, constantly threw pranks around the school. Let's just say his reputation didn't give me a good one since we carried the same last name." He rolls his eyes. "But anyway, that's when I started really getting into music. I guess it was my form of therapy and it just stuck with me."

"And now look at you; you're about to be on the road to making a career out of it," I say before I take another bite of my food.

"Yeah, I hate the phrase *everything happens for a reason*,

but sometimes it's hard not to believe, no matter whether you want to believe it or not." He slides closer to me in the booth a bit. "That's kind of why I asked you out at the diner. Honestly, I never really do that. I'm never that confident but I don't know," he pauses, "coincidentally meeting twice, two days in a row, I just had to ask you out."

"Yeah," I smile. "I did find it weird that we ran into each other again. Michelle called it fate," I roll my eyes. "I never really thought about whether I believed in fate or not until she said it."

"Whether fate or the phrase that I hate is true, I'm just glad that I had the courage to ask you out. I was pretty nervous," he chuckles.

"Nervous?" I gasp as I scrunch my forehead. "You were so confident when you asked me! I didn't think you were nervous at all!"

"Over falsification of confidence is the key to sounding confident," he grins.

"Fake it until you make it," I agree just as the music starts to get louder which breaks our attention off each other and to the band.

"Not bad, huh?" Max asks as he scoots his body closer to me and puts his arm around my shoulders.

"Yeah, not bad at all," I agree. "They're pretty good. How did you find out about them?"

"They had a flyer on the bulletin board in school. Actually, it was on the board where we first met. I looked their profile up to hear their music when I left. I thought they sounded pretty good, so I wanted to come see them with you."

"Oh, I thought you said you weren't on social media?" I innocently ask.

"Oh, I'm not at all," he shakes his head. "I just looked them up to see if they sounded good. Like I said before, I kind of hate the internet. I don't judge people that post about their lives, but I personally like to keep mine private. I have nothing really fascinating about my life to show anyway," he pauses. "I know... that probably makes me sound weird, but I promise you that I'm not a serial killer or in the witness protection program."

I bust out laughing. "I wasn't thinking either of those things, but Michelle might be. I'll admit, we both already tried to stalk you online already... Well, I did before you told me you didn't have it. Michelle, on the other hand, might still be looking for you," I giggle.

"I'm not surprised or offended by it," Max laughs back.

About half an hour later, the band ended their set on stage, then we left and took the train back to Forest Hill. It's a quarter past midnight and being the gentlemen that Max is, he is walking me up to my apartment door. I was kind of expecting that he would do this again but at the same time, I was also not sure of how we were going to end the night. Even though it is only our second date, it feels like I have known him a lot longer than I have. I feel comfortable with him... but that also feels weird to me because we just met. I wasn't even this comfortable when Nate and I started dating at first... and we knew each other for at least two years before we even got together.

However, regardless of my feelings right now, I know I can't let my anxiety control me. I do need to move on with my life. It's been a whole four months since my breakup anyway and I was starting to get over it before my accident. I need to continue doing that. I think about how Nate was really messing with my mentality before, and I can't believe that I was actually wasting so many weeks crying over him... so many weeks leading up to my coma.

"I had a great time again tonight," Max says as he towers over me at my door.

"Me too," I smile. "I've never been on a date in the city. It was really nice," I admit to him.

"I'm glad we went," he agrees.

"Me too," I mumble again as I try to remain eye contact with him.

He leans into me, holding both my hands together before he looks down into my eyes and in the next second, I feel his lips on mine.

"Good night, Jen," he says after our lips part a moment later.

"Good night," I gulp, hoping that my face isn't beat red before I turn to walk inside of my apartment.

I had no plans to start dating someone right now, especially while I am pre-occupied in finding the driver that hit me, but I think Max might be a good distraction. For the first time in months, I'm actually starting to feel a sense of happiness again and it's because of Max. I would probably be way more consumed in my own investigation which I know isn't good for me because the last thing that I want, is to let the other driver keep controlling my life. They already fucked up my head. I'm not going to let them ruin my love life too.

I've never thought about whether fate exists or not, and I'm not sure if Michelle believes it does either or if she was just trying to get me laid, but now I can't seem to get the damn word out of my head.

CHAPTER 9

I just woke up to see a missed call from my mom already. It's only a few minutes past noon. Instead of calling her back right away, I am making myself some coffee first. After I got home from my date with Max last night, it was hard to fall asleep because I was replaying every moment between us in my head. I think it was sometime between 3:00 and 3:30 a.m. when I ended up finally falling asleep.

While I'm waiting for it to finish brewing, my eyes catch sight of the hospital bill on my kitchen floor. I never picked it up after I threw it the other day during my outburst of rage, and I am not interested to look at it again, but I know I need to sooner or later... so, I might as well do it now.

When I pick it up, I instantly become aggravated once I see that $2,000.00 amount due in the corner. I understand that nothing can really be free in life, but what I don't understand is why I am being charged such a large amount even though I have health insurance. I thought that having health insurance was supposed to cover large bills, not make me owe them. I am hoping that this is a mistake or there's a way that I can at least get the amount knocked down, so I decide to call my health insurance company.

After a few rings, an operating system answers, then I

select the option to speak with a representative before I set my phone on speaker. I leave it on the kitchen counter, and I begin to clean up my house while I wait for someone to answer.

Fifteen minutes later, the waiting music cuts off from the phone, so I rush out from the bathroom where I had been wiping down my sink with cleaner. "Hello! Hi. Yes, hold on!" I call out as I practically trip over my own two feet. "Hi, my name's Jennifer Russo. I'm calling about a bill that I received from the hospital. I'd like to know if it was a mistake or if I could possibly do something about the amount that is owed."

The insurance agent asks me for my social security number and date of birth to confirm my identity, then a moment passes before he says, "Okay, I'm looking at your account now. The amount that is billed to you is due because that is what was left of the remainder from your deductible."

"My what?" I question.

"Your deductible," he answers. "Your health plan has a $2,000 annual deductible which is what comes out of your pocket. This is used so the insurance can take care of the rest of your healthcare expenses."

"Okay... but why am I being charged that amount specifically? I don't understand."

"Because that is what came with the plan you chose, ma'am. Lower deductible plans are more costly monthly, and the higher deductible plans are less costly per month. Did you choose your plan based off of the monthly cost?"

Yes. My cheap ass did. "Uh, yeah. I guess I did," I groan. "So, the whole amount is due in three months?" I ask even though I see it plain on the paper in front of me.

"Yes. If you think you are going to have trouble paying

it, then I suggest that you call the billing department of the hospital. They'll most likely be able to work out a payment plan with you."

I thank the insurance agent and hang up, then I call the number on the hospital bill. I select three unnecessary options to try to reach someone until I finally hear a woman's voice over my speaker about ten minutes later. After she pulls my account up, the first question that she asks is, "Are you calling to make a payment on your account today?"

"Uh, no," I scoff unintendedly. "I'm calling to understand why I am being charged the amount that I am."

"It says here that the amount you are being charged is the amount after your deduct-"

"My deductible. Yes. I was told that," I interrupt her. "But what exactly is this charge for? I need some clarification, please."

"You are being billed the remainder of what the cost of your hospital stay was. You stayed a total of two weeks. Your insurance only covered a portion of it."

Did she just call my two weeks of being a coma patient like it was a vacation? During one week of that time, I was practically dead and during the other, I was begging to leave... and now they are expecting me to pay for being there, like it was my choice?

"My stay? I didn't choose to *stay* there for a week. I didn't choose to go to the hospital at all," I say in a confused tone.

"I'm sorry ma'am, but that's just what your insurance plan included. We can work out a payment plan if you would like," she answers.

"Okay. Well, what kind of payment plan?" I irritably

ask, as I know there is really no use in arguing with her as it will probably just get me angrier.

"The lowest amount I can do is $200.00 per month. If you make the minimum payment each month, you should have it paid off within ten months."

Two hundred dollars? After my rent and utility bills, I'm usually left with about two hundred and fifty dollars a month which I normally use for savings, gas, and food. If I add an extra two hundred dollars to my monthly bills, I'll have barely any spending money and I won't be able to save for another car either.

"I-I, uh, okay. I'll have to call you back after I go over my finances," I say before I end the call without even saying thank you or goodbye, then I begin to play some music on my phone to keep myself calm. Seconds later, my phone rings. I don't recognize the number that's calling but it's a Forest Hill area code, so I answer anyways. "Hello?" I question in a curious tone.

"Hi Jen. This is Natalie. You left me your number the other day at my house. I told you that I'd have my husband check our camera outside."

"Oh, hi!" My voice becomes perky. I didn't expect her to actually call me back. "Do you still have the footage?"

"Yeah, you're actually in luck. My husband told me that the footage automatically deletes every thirty days. Another few days, and we would not have had it anymore. You told me September 20th after 11:00 p.m. right?"

"Yes! Did you see a truck pass by?" I gasp excitedly.

"We saw two trucks pass by around the time but only one of them had a headlight out like you described. We played back the footage a few times, but we could only see the first few letters on the license plate. I think they are the letters; T, E and A, but I'm not entirely sure. The camera is too far away from the street so I can't really see the plate well."

"Oh my god! This is actually really helpful. Would you mind taking a picture of it and texting it to me?" I ask and Natalie does not mind at all. I thank her again before we hang up, and I receive her text message a minute later.

The resolution of her security cameras photo is extra difficult to see, probably because it's a photo of a video, so I still can't see the plate number clearly. I do know that this truck on her camera is definitely the same one that the store and the other guy's camera caught. Natalie said that the third letter looks like the letter A, but I think it looks more like the number eight. I need to find someone else who might have caught this truck on camera, so I can see the whole license plate better. Then, I should be able to go to the DMV and see who owns it or possibly look the plate up online myself. I have not actually thoroughly thought my whole plan through yet but at least I'm getting somewhere right now. At least this is a start.

I look at the photo again, then I swipe over to the videos in my phone to replay them. The only damage that I can see on the truck is the smashed hood and left headlight. I would think that since my car got completely totaled, then their vehicle had to have taken some more damage than what I can see.

Then again, maybe it didn't because the person was able to drive away... but, who is to say that the truck didn't stall out further down the road after it hit me or maybe something else happened to it during the crash, that might have affected it? Regardless of how much damage the pickup truck sustained, I would think that the driver would probably want to get the truck fixed... *unless they got rid of the vehicle instead.* I'm sure there are a ton of ways to get rid of a vehicle around here, but I wouldn't know any since I'm not a criminal.

However, if the driver of the truck wanted to get it fixed then maybe, they took it to a mechanic shop... or what if they wanted to get rid of it and junked it?

I decide to search the internet for all the mechanics and junkyards listed in Forest Hill. There are five auto shops and two junkyards that show in the results. Out of the list, I've only been to Larry's Auto because my dad usually takes our cars there. Even though I can't afford to miss anymore work, I'm going to call in sick, then I'm going to drive to the mechanic shops and junkyards instead.

As I grab my keys and head out my door, I call the salon and ask for my manager. "Hey, it's Jen. Is Angie in?" I ask Kelly, the other receptionist who I am supposed to take over for, when she answers the phone.

"No not yet," Kelly says in a worrisome voice.

I think she knows that I'm about to call out.

"Alright, well can you tell her that I'm not feeling well. My heads killing me. I think I need to rest for the day. I don't think it's a good idea for me to go into work," I say.

A few seconds pass before I hear Kelly sigh. "Alright. I'll tell her. Feel better."

I know that I probably pissed her off because my boss is most likely going to ask her to cover my shift, but I don't care about that right now. Although, I don't like that I'm using my brain injury as a lie, I know that telling her the truth about what I'm really going to do wouldn't have been more excusable.

Fifteen minutes later, I arrive at Larry's Auto which is attached to a gas station on the south end of Forest. There are four mechanics outside when I park my car. As soon as I step out, they all turn their attention toward me.

"Can I help you?" The older looking mechanic asks as he walks right up to my car.

"Uh, yeah…" I pause as once again; I did not actually think about what I was going to say. "I'm looking to see if my boyfriend's pickup truck is finished. He brought it in a few weeks ago. It had a broken left headlight."

"You sure he brought it here? The only trucks we got right now are what you see behind me and none of them are here for a broken light," he says as he looks over toward the open garage.

I follow his gaze over to see one pickup truck up on a car lift and its bright red. Two more trucks sit outside in the parking lot, and they are yellow and white. None of them look like what's on the security cameras. *But what if the truck was already taken care of here and I'm just too late? After all, it has been weeks since my accident already, so it could be a possibility.*

"Oh, hm," I pause. "Well, maybe he picked it up already and forgot to tell me. Uh, do you happen to remember working on a truck for a missing light or a dented hood recently? I'm just trying to surprise him when he gets home, so I don't want to call to ask him where he dropped it off. I might be a little late on the surprise though." I clear my throat as I am not confident in my quick lie at all.

The guy is giving me a peculiar look. "Can't say I do," he shakes his head, "but I can tell you that most of our customers here are regulars. We get very few newbies. What's your boyfriend's name? I can look it up to see if he's come in here before."

Shit… again, I didn't think this far. I haven't been thinking anything through at all. I don't even know where this magical boyfriend lie had even come from. I probably should have told him the truth, but I panicked and now it's too late. Giving this guy a fake boyfriend name is not going to help me since he doesn't exist. I scan the garage with my eyes once more before I say, "It's okay. Never mind. I'll just give him a call. Thank you anyways."

I leave Larry's and I head to the second mechanic shop on the list, Carter Auto. As soon as I park, I immediately get a weird vibe from the place. It is an open standalone auto garage a few blocks away from Larry's and there are a few mechanics around. I just counted six of them. This garage is twice as busier and bigger than Larry's.

I get out of my car and walk toward the office door, but I am stopped by two mechanics almost right away. "Hi, can we help you?"

"Yeah, maybe," I pause while I decide whether to use my fake boyfriend excuse or to tell him the truth. "Uh, I am looking for a pickup truck that might've been dropped off here for a busted left headlight."

"Is this truck that you're looking for *yours*, honey?" One of the mechanics asks with a raised eyebrow and a smirk on his face.

"Uh, no," I press my lips. If I tell them that my fake boyfriend brought it in, they are probably going to ask me for his name like the guy at Larry's did. "Well, to be honest, I don't know whose truck it is that I'm looking for," I say as I pull up the video from the guys house on my phone and show it to them. "I'm looking for this truck. The driver crashed into me weeks ago and sent me into a coma. They fled the scene, and the cops have not found them. I've been doing some investigating myself, so I thought I'd come here to see if maybe the person that owns it dropped it off to get it fixed," I sigh. "Then I could figure out who the driver is."

The two men are looking down at me with a

scrutinizing look on their faces when one of them says, "When did this accident of yours happen?"

"About three weeks ago," I answer. I don't like the way they are beginning to look at me. Offense and contemplation show on their face which is making me highly uncomfortable.

"You don't look like you were in a coma," the other mechanic says. By the tone in his voice, either these guys either don't believe me, or they find my story amusing.

"Well, I most definitely was," I snap back as I force a fake smile.

The other mechanic leans in closer to my phone to look at the screen once more, then looks over at the guy next him and they both laugh. "Honey, we wouldn't have a car sitting here for that long if it just had a broken headlight."

"Oh, well… as you can see the hood had some damage on it too," I say as I begin to play the video on my phone and hold it out to show them.

The guys both look at each other and smirk again. "A hood doesn't take three weeks either, dear," the same guy answers while the other one is shaking his head.

I guess they are right. I know absolutely nothing about cars but fixing a headlight and a hood probably can't take more than a few days. It's been weeks since my accident so why would I think it would still be here?

Although the mechanic makes sense, I don't thank his condescending ass, and I get back in my car. Once I'm in, I immediately lock my doors. I can see a few guys in the garage eyeing me from the distance, which is making me feel even more uneasy, so I quickly turn on the ignition, and speed out of the parking lot.

I'm a good mile away now. I can slow down. *I need to stop being so paranoid.* As I drive, I think about when I told the convenient store manager my story. She was willing to help me but that was only because she said she had prior problems with the police, so I guess I got lucky. I thought those guys just now would be a little bit more sensitive to my story, but I was very wrong which makes me not want to go to the other mechanic shops around here.

Instead, I am going to check out the two junkyards that came up in the list. Those aren't mechanic places so I shouldn't have to question anybody or answer anyone's questions either. I should be able to just look around the yard on my own. Depending on what I find, then I might drive to the rest of the shops after that.

I arrive to the first place - Juncker's Junkyard, which is about the equivalent size of a two-pump gas station and convenient store including its parking lot. A chain link fence with barb wire on the top of it surrounds the perimeter of the yard. When I get out of my car and walk toward the office, I stop to look through the fence behind it. I can see pretty much almost all the vehicles behind the fence and there aren't many. There are a few sedan cars and a couple SUVs, but I don't see any pickup trucks from where I am standing. However, I still walk into the office anyway.

There is a skinny man with reading glasses on sitting behind a desk. He is looking at his computer in front of him. "Hello, can I help you?" His voice is raspy when he speaks.

"Hello. I am just coming in here to check out some parts in your yard," I say.

"What are you looking for?"

Crap... I wasn't prepared for that question.

"Uh," I pause as I try to quickly think. "Um, I'm just

looking for a new passenger door for my beamer."

The guy gives me a meaningful grin. "Well, I can tell you right now that most of the doors on the vehicles are probably not so salvageable," he pauses as he looks me up and down, "and if they are, you're going to need my help when taking it off the car and carrying it since I don't think you have any tools in that purse," he says as he stands up from behind his desk and begins to walk out of the office. "Follow me. I'll help you," he volunteers, and I reluctantly follow him into the lot of cars.

I was hoping that I could just roam off on my own, but this guy is being so friendly that I don't want to be rude and tell him to fuck off, even though it is on the tip of my tongue.

"Alright, I got one beamer here," he says as we pass a white older version of my BMW. "You can see the passenger door is pretty dented in though. I don't think that will work for you. Let's check the other two ones I got. Follow me."

As I'm following about a foot behind him, I look around the property for any pickup trucks. I'm glad that I decided to walk into the office because I didn't know that there were more vehicles lined up on the other side of the building where he is leading me right now. I notice a pickup truck backed up against the fence but the color of it is white and it has a cab on top of the bed. The headlights aren't broken either. I don't think that's it, so I don't bother to check it out.

We take a left into another row of cars when I spot a black pickup amongst the other vehicles. The hood looks like it is minorly bent, the front windshield is busted out, and it is missing its driver door. I pull out my phone from my purse and look at the photo in my text from Natalie.

The truck in front of me down the road, has a cab over the bed but the one on the security camera does not. Although, I barely know a thing about vehicles, I know that cabs on the back of pickup trucks can be removed easily. What if the driver didn't have the cab on their truck that night?

"Just as I figured, these doors will do you no good either. Missing handles," the man's voice breaks my focus from the truck ahead.

I look at the beamer in front of me and sigh. "Damn... So that's all you've got here?" I shift my feet as I try to figure out how to transition over to the truck ahead.

"Sorry, ma'am. That's all we got," he half smiles.

"Uh, it's okay," I hesitate before I begin to just walk directly toward the truck. "What kind of truck is this over here? My dad mentioned that he was looking for some parts to fix up his F-150," I lie.

"Oh, this is a Ford Ranger. It's been here a while," I hear him say as he follows behind me.

"How long has it been here?" I walk around it to look for a license plate, but I don't see one. "Oh, for at least a few years now. Any of the vehicles that are up against the fence have been here the longest. The newer ones are in the front rows."

If he's telling the truth... which I'm pretty sure he is, then this truck is not the one. It does look like it's been sitting here for a lot longer than a couple weeks anyway.

"Alright, well thank you for your time," I sigh as I start to walk back toward the entrance since I don't see any more pickup trucks anywhere. When I get back in my car, I head straight to the next junkyard on Coolidge Street.

It took me only ten minutes to drive over. The guy in the front office asked me what I am looking for and this time I was more prepared for the question. I said that I was looking for a new rearview mirror because I realized that needing a door requires help from someone since I clearly don't have any tools with me, and I don't want any help. Thankfully unlike the guy at Juncker's, this guy was not as friendly and didn't invite himself to tag along. He only had me show him my driver's license and then he let me right through to the yard by myself.

This junkyard is a lot more organized than Juncker's and it's twice as big. This one is also surrounded by at least a six-foot-tall wooden fence. I knew the yard looked fairly big when I first pulled in, but I didn't expect the lot to be filled with so many rows of different vehicles. Some vehicles are stacked on top of each other on double car lifts while piles of car parts line the fence on the ground.

I head down the first row, passing four trucks, but they are all so wrecked that I can barely tell what they looked like before. If the truck that hit me is any one of them, then there is absolutely no way that I would be able to compare them to what is on the security footage. I continue to maneuver through the next two rows of vehicles and venture deeper into the lot.

After passing through and only seeing a few more trucks, I decide that none of them could be the one I am looking for and I continue down the fifth row. Halfway down, I see a dark blue F-150 pickup. All four doors are missing, the left headlight is busted while the right is intact, and the hood is dented in. I walk behind it to look at the license plate but there isn't one. I pull out my phone and examine the picture that Natalie sent, then I replay the two videos.

Besides the fact that all four doors are missing on the truck in front of me, the truck on the security cameras looks almost identical to it. This truck here, isn't placed in the back of the junkyard either. It's only a few rows in and there's at least six or more rows after it... I wonder if this junkyard operates the same way as Juncker's does. It would only make sense; newer cars would be placed in the front of the yard and older cars would be more toward the back.

Even though, I know that it would be *way* too much of a coincidence for me to just find the truck like this, I walk around it and take a ten second video with my phone anyways. Then I take a picture too. Just as I do, I get a text message from Max.

It reads - **Morning! I had fun with you again last night. I'm off work today. If you're free, would you like to meet me for a late lunch in an hour?**

I want to say yes but I also want to say no. I desperately have the urge to keep up my search right now, but I also don't want to turn Max down. Being with him makes me comfortable and happy... which I like. I don't remember the last time that I felt happy even before my accident happened because I had been dealing with Nate's drama then. I decide to text Max back that I would love to have lunch with him, and we decide to meet in an hour and a half.

I should probably stop obsessing over looking for this asshole and go back home to get ready to meet Max... but before I leave, I need to ask the guy at the desk if he can tell me who brought this truck in, just for my own peace of mind. I know there are other trucks out here and more rows that I can look through, but my stubborn ass needs to still ask about this one. The similarities between them are too coincidental for me. Plus, I don't have time to keep searching through the yard right now anyways.

"Find what you needed?" the man asks when I walk into the office.

"Hi. Yes, I think I might have," I say. "I saw a blue F-150 in the lot. I was wondering if you know when that was brought in?"

He furrows his eyebrows. "Oh, I'd have to look up the VIN number and registration on it to figure that out. Why are you asking? I thought you told me that you came here to look for a rear-view mirror."

"Right…" I pause as I shift my feet nervously on the ground. "Well, I'm actually not here to look for a mirror. I'm looking for a specific pickup truck that might've been brought in a few weeks ago-"

"Why are you looking for it?" He cuts me off as he stands up from behind the desk. Like the guys at the auto shop, his face just became tense which makes me re-think telling him the truth. That one mechanic laughed at me when I said I was in a coma and this guy's face is giving off the same vibes. I don't want to get the same reaction, so I quickly use my imaginary boyfriend lie again.

"Uh, well my boyfriend's truck was stolen, and we've been looking everywhere for it. He's at work right now so I figured I'd stop by here to help him find it… That blue truck looks like it could be it, but I can't really tell because of the damages and the plate is gone. I thought maybe whoever stole it, might've junked it or something."

He crosses his arms against his chest. "Well, I can tell you that every vehicle that is brought in here is brought in by the owner and are registered with clean titles. We don't take anything without those things. If someone tried to bring a stolen truck in here, then I would know about it."

By the way he just answered, I think I offended him. I

thought lying about a crime would do better than telling the truth about one but clearly, I was wrong. I have nothing more to say to him, so I just thank him and walk away. Even if I told him the truth, just by his demeanor alone, I don't think he would've reacted any differently toward me. I really want to keep driving around for more clues but instead, I head home. I need to quickly shower and change into something cuter than these old worn-out jeans before I go meet Max for lunch.

—

I chose to wear a pair of dark blue jeans, a baby blue colored V-neck long sleeve and my black ankle high, thick heeled boots, to meet Max for lunch. We decided to meet at Rosie's Cafe which has vintage like outdoor seating. I put my hair up into a high ponytail and pushed my bangs back with a black hairband so they would not look insanely wild in the wind while I eat. We are sitting at a two-seater table on the sidewalk right outside of Rosie's windows. I picked this place since it's in the same plaza as Stoney's, so I could walk over. Max and I met here only about twenty minutes ago, and our food just arrived at our table.

"So, how's your day going?" he asks before he takes a bite of his burger.

"It's alright," I answer as I choose to not go into detail about what I was really doing. "How's yours?"

"Pretty good," he nods his head as he finishes a bite of his food. "Honestly, I woke up about an hour before I called you. I had a few beers with my brother last night. I didn't get to bed until about three in the morning."

"That's around the time that I think I went to bed too, but I wasn't drinking," I say. "I just couldn't sleep. I fell in the Netflix rabbit hole for a few hours."

"That'll get ya," he agrees. "Yeah, my brother can be a bit of a bad influence sometimes," he laughs. "Do you have any brothers or sisters?"

I shake my head, no. "I wish I do sometimes, though. Being an only child is kind of lonely," I sort of chuckle a bit. "Even as an adult."

"Eh, siblings are fun until they aren't," he laughs as he pulls his phone out of his jean pocket. "So, did you get your class schedule yet? Mine was emailed this morning. I got night classes Tuesday through Friday."

"Oh, I haven't even checked yet. I forgot that it would be ready today," I say as I pull out my phone from my purse to look at my email. I've been so wrapped up in investigating my accident that I haven't thought about starting college in nearly two weeks. I'm not prepared for it at all.

"I have night classes on Tuesday through Thursday but on Friday, I have a morning class," I answer as I look at my schedule.

"So, we're both taking classes on the same days?" he grins.

"I guess so," I smile and tilt my head. "You were saying everything happens for a reason."

"I did say that, didn't I?" He flashes me a wide smile before taking a sip of his soda. "I heard that there is going to be a carnival this weekend. Do you want to go with me Friday night?"

"Oh sure," I answer, leaving out the fact that I've been there plenty of times and I'm kind of over going by now. Forest Hill's annual carnival is held every October on the property of the biggest church in our city, Trinity church. I would usually go with Nate and the rest of my friend's every year during high school but ever since we graduated, we all been kind of separate and I don't think any of us plan to really hang out there again. I haven't even talked to anybody besides Michelle since my breakup anyway.

Max has only been living in Forest Hill for a year. He's clearly never gone to the carnival here and by the look on his face, he looks too excited to take me so, I won't say no to him. I like being with him and even if I'm experiencing something I've done already, it will still be a new experience with him... just like how we went downtown together. "I've been there a few times," I tell him. "But I'd still love to go with you. It should be fun."

Just as I go to take a sip of my soda, the sudden sounds of squealing tires followed by a loud crash makes me drop my drink. The cup is plastic, so it doesn't break but my soda spills all over the table and a bit onto my lap. I can feel the soda dripping on me from the table but I'm not reacting to it. I'm not moving at all. I can't stand up or speak. I'm only staring at the two cars that just crashed into each other at the intersection ahead of us. I didn't see the crash happen, but I caught the aftermath of it.

It looks like the car that was making a left turn at the light got T-boned by the other car that was driving in the opposite direction. A young woman, who looks not that much older than me, just stumbled out of the driver seat of the T-boned car but by the looks of her body language, she doesn't seem injured. She just looks like she's panicking hard. Watching her walk away from her car and over to the other driver, then seeing that other person get out with no injuries also, makes me wish that I had done the same thing during my accident.

"Jen," Max reaches over to my right arm and gently touches it with his fingertips. "Are you okay?"

"Uh. Yeah, I'm -- I'm fine," I stutter. I can feel a sense of panic starting to run through me and I'm not sure why. My chest is feeling tight, like I'm on the edge of a panic attack which is irritating me because there's no reason for me to panic right now.

"Do you want to take our food to go? We can finish eating in the park," Max says, and I notice that he is cleaning up the table with some napkins.

I feel like an idiot for dropping my drink, and I feel even more embarrassed that I'm on the verge of tears and hyperventilation right now. I want to continue our lunch, but I can't sit here with those cars in my view. *I can't stop looking.* "Uh, yeah. If you don't mind," I answer, then clear my throat to try to mask the shakiness in my voice.

Max signals for the waiter to ask for the check along with two to-go boxes. When the waiter comes back, Max immediately hands him a ten and a twenty-dollar bill, then tells him to keep the change before putting our food into the boxes. The next thing I know, Max is escorting me away from the table and is walking me down the street in the opposite direction of the accident.

Once we are just a few feet down the sidewalk, he wraps his arms around my shoulders, and I begin to calm down as we walk down the street to finish our lunch at the park.

CHAPTER 10

Once I got home from my lunch date with Max, I ended up taking a long nap and fell asleep for the rest of the day. Since then, I haven't had any time to continue my search for the truck because I've been staying an hour later at work every day for the past few days to make some extra money. I wanted to look for the truck after work today, but I didn't have time because I had to get ready to go to the carnival with Max.

Surprisingly after my panic attack at Rosie's, he still showed up to my apartment and took me out tonight. I honestly thought that I freaked him out, but he was so calm after we left the cafe and it helped me stop panicking as soon as we got to the park. He distracted me completely by talking about our college plans which made me feel better.

We just got to the carnival a little while ago. I am waiting for him to get us some drinks and pretzels while I sit at one of the picnic tables set up around the food trucks. There are a lot of people here and barely any empty tables, so I rushed over to sit down as soon as I saw one open.

"Jen?" My heart feels like it drops to my feet when I hear my name and recognize the voice. I look up from my cell phone to see Nate in front of my table. He is wearing a backward baseball cap as he usually does, along with a blue hoodie and jeans.

"It's good to see you," he says as he looks through me with his piercing blue eyes.

"Mhmm," I mumble. "Yeah, you too." Talking to Nate is difficult for me now. He wasn't just my boyfriend; he was my *first boyfriend,* and I was in love with him. But that all changed when I found out that he slept with someone else. I said that I would never forgive him, and I made a promise to hold myself to it, no matter how deep he looks at me with his blue eyes.

"Listen, Jen. I just wanted to tell you that I came to visit you while you were..." he pauses.

"Dead. I was dead," I say, finishing his sentence with a smirk.

"You always have to be so morbid," he sighs and rolls his eyes.

One thing, Nate and I always argued about was how dark and pessimistic I can be sometimes. He is the complete opposite. He always sees the brighter picture no matter what the situation is. I don't intend to sound negative, but I just normally see the realistic side of things and sometimes it's not always positive. I think it's good to acknowledge that.

"Anyway, I just wanted to tell you that I was there. You really scared me. I'm glad you're okay now." As he finishes his sentence, I see Max walking up behind him with two drinks and pretzels in his hands. Nate notices me looking past his shoulder and turns around to look in the same direction. "Wait? Who are you here with? Where is Michelle?" he asks as he turns back to me.

"I'm not here with Michelle. I'm actually here with Max," I say just as Max approaches the table.

"Everything okay here?" Max asks in a concerning, yet

still calm tone while he sets down the drinks and pretzels on the table before taking a seat across from me.

"Yup," I nod. "Um, Max this is Nate. Nate this is Max."

"Sup' man?" Max nods and Nate nods back.

"Nate was just leaving," I say as I look right into Nate's eyes.

"She's right," Nate says as he looks at me, then looks at Max.

I can't tell if the look on his face is showing hurt, confusion, or if he's surprised that I'm here with another guy. Either way, I don't care. I just want him to leave right now. *I feel awkward.*

"Have a good night. It was nice seeing you again, Jen," he says, then turns and walks away.

"So, who's Nate?" Max nonchalantly asks before taking a bite of his pretzel.

"My ex-boyfriend. We broke up a few months ago," I sigh. I can feel my heart still slightly racing. I wasn't prepared for any of that.

"Was that awkward for you?" Max chuckles.

"How'd you know?" I raise my eyebrows.

"Your face right now," he grins.

I roll my eyes as I feel my cheeks grow red, "Oh yeah, well… I haven't seen him in a while," I sigh. "He cheated on me."

Max's eyebrows raise as he stops smiling. He looks back behind him in the direction that Nate walked, then turns around back toward me. "Well, if I knew that, then I wouldn't have sup' manned him then."

I start laughing. "You make me smile," I say and immediately feel embarrassed when the words leave my mouth.

He doesn't laugh but gives me a genuine smile. "Good,

you make me smile too. So, I have a confession," he pauses. "I'm kind of scared to go on some of these rides."

"Seriously?" I look at him in disbelief.

"Hey! Don't make fun of me. I just don't like the really fast ones," he shrugs.

"Then, why did you invite me here?" I ask.

"I don't know," he says as he shrugs again. "I thought it would be something different to do for a date. I wanted to take you somewhere fun."

I slightly blush when he speaks. The fact that he took me to a place that he does not even like, just because he wanted to do something different and fun to impress me, means a lot to me. "Well, then I have an idea. Are you afraid of heights?" I ask.

"As long as they aren't moving quickly, then I'm good," he says, then raises an eyebrow as I stand up with my pretzel and drink in my hands. "Why?"

"I have a surprise. Follow me." I go to walk away from the table, and he follows my lead.

"Woah, where are we going? I didn't mean we had to leave," he says as we walk out of the entrance of the carnival.

"I know that!" I giggle and continue walking. I lead him into the parking lot and to the side of the church building before I stop in front of a line of bushes. I take a second to look around us before I duck down quickly and crawl through them. "Come on!" I whisper.

"What are we doing?" Max is questioning my moves in a whisper as well, but he's still following me.

"Just trust me," I tell him as I take his pretzel. I wrap it in a napkin before putting it in my purse, along with mine. Then, I carefully climb up with my drink in one hand, onto the slope of the roof, which is only about an inch taller than me from the ground. "Be careful," I whisper.

He follows me as we both crawl the slope up to the top where the Holy Cross sculpture is sitting directly in the middle of the roof. We sit at the edge of it, and I pull our pretzels back out of my purse so we can finish eating. We can see the entire view of the carnival from here and it's beautiful.

"I thought eating up here would be better than eating down there," I say as I hand him his pretzel.

"Wow," he says in awe of the carnival view.

"Told you to trust me," I say as I admire the view myself. I've seen it so many other times before because my friend's and I used to come up here but seeing it with Max feels different. I never even came up here with Nate alone. We were always with other people.

Max slides his arm around me after we finish eating and I rest my head on his shoulder. As we sit in silence and we take in the view, I feel at peace in his arms. I feel like I don't have to worry. I'm not even nervous. At first, I was hesitant on dating at this time in my life, but I like this feeling with Max... *happiness.*

His fingers are running up and down my shoulder blade which is causing tiny goosebumps to appear on my skin. I feel his fingertips moving from my shoulder down my back and I nuzzle my head into his neck.

"This is perfect," he whispers. I lift my head up from his chest to look at him. He looks down at me and connects his lips with mine. I lean into his body as we continue to kiss, my legs now sideways over his lap. Fireworks startle us minutes later and we break free of each other.

After about ten minutes of fireworks, we went back into the carnival and walked around, just talking to each other and laughing at the people's reactions on the rides before we decided to leave.

We just walked into my building and like at the end of our dates; Max is walking me all the way to my front door. "I had fun tonight," he says as we approach my apartment.

"Me too," I gulp. I can feel my heart racing.

He reaches down to kiss me, and my lips fall deep into his. Seconds later we break free, but Max continues holding me around my waist. Instead of letting me go and walking away, he lingers for a moment, keeping our eyes locked on each other's. I reach up once more to kiss him and he moves his hands from my waist to hold both of mine while we do. Our lips part again and this time, I don't let go.

I didn't realize I was turning around to unlock my front door while still holding on to one of his hands until I step in my doorway, leading him in with me.

I turn to lock the door behind us, then he spins me around, pushing my back up against the door. His lips meet mine as he slides his hands gently up the back of my shirt. I help him in lifting it over my head, our lips meeting again before I start to lead him down the hallway to my bedroom.

—

Waking up next to Max this morning feels surreal as he lays next to me, still sound asleep. I don't know where the confidence in me came from when I brought him into my apartment last night... but it was like our eyes were telling each other that we both didn't want to let go, and I just... reacted.

"Do you like watching me sleep?" I embarrassingly

jump at the sound of his voice. "I like when you blush," he says before reaching over to kiss me on my forehead.

I give him a half smile while I rub the scar on the back of my head. I can feel a slight headache coming on and I know I should probably go take my medication soon. Max must have noticed my face because he has a concerned expression. "What's wrong? Is your head hurting?"

This wasn't how I planned on telling him about my coma, but I feel like now is the only moment. I've been dodging the subject, but I don't want to *not* tell him about it. That's not a good way to start off a relationship, with lies. That is… if this is even turning into a relationship. *At least, I hope it is.* I mean, I feel like we are moving quickly but I don't feel like that is a bad thing because I also feel really comfortable with him.

"Uh, no. Actually, it's not," I sigh. "Okay, so remember when I told you that I got my broken arm from a car accident when I was going to Michelle's apartment?"

Max nods his head, yes.

"Well, I didn't only break my arm," I pause. "The accident sent me into a coma for a week, and I had just got out of it right before we met. I didn't tell you this yet because I didn't really want to talk about it. I hate even thinking about it." I pull my hair up from my neck and show him my scar.

"I noticed this, but I didn't want to ask," he says as he rubs his finger gently over it. "Does it hurt?"

"No. It doesn't hurt when you touch it, but I still get these headaches every now and then. I can feel one coming on right now. I have medicine for it."

"Is that what the scar on your forehead is from?"

As I nod my head, my cell phone rings on my nightstand. "Ugh, I bet it's my mother," I sigh as I reach over and grab it. "I should answer her. Ever since the accident, she's been extra clingy."

Max's face untenses as he slightly chuckles. "No problem. I'll let you have some privacy. You know, you're very strong to go through what you did, baby. That must've been a horrible experience for you. You can tell me more after you get off the phone. Want me to make us some coffee?" he asks as he grabs his clothes off the floor.

"That'd be great," I smile, and he leaves the room. I'm pleasantly surprised at Max's response to hearing I was in a coma. His eyes didn't grow wide, and he didn't ask me a million questions or even doubt that I was in one, like the mechanics did. Instead, he just acted like his usual calm self which is just what I wanted and hoped would happen.

"Hi, mom," I say when I answer my phone.

"Hi, honey. How are you feeling?"

"Still not dead."

There's a pause as I can picture her shaking her head and rolling her eyes behind the phone. "Okay, I get it. I'll stop asking you that question," she says. "What are you doing today? Can I come over?"

"Um, no, not today. I'm actually hanging out with someone new. His name is Max."

"Oh, that's great! Is he cute?" My mom gasps in excitement. She loved Nate until she learned that he cheated on me.

"Yes," I laugh. "I first met him when I was enrolling in school the other day."

"When do I get to meet him?"

"Mom, I just met him." I wish she could see me rolling my eyes. "I love you, but I have to go now. I just woke up. I'll call you tomorrow, okay?"

"Okay, call me if you need anything! Love you," she

says as she usually ends every phone call with me, always emphasizing the *call me* part.

"Love you, too." I hang up and put on my robe.

When I walk out to the smell of the coffee brewing, I hear the shower running from my bathroom, so I go toward it. I walk in and see that Max is about to step into the shower. When he sees me, he stops and smiles.

"Want to join me?" he asks as he wraps his hands around my waist, and I let him take my robe off me.

—

After our shower, Max and I were both running late for work, so we quickly drank our coffee and Max just walked me to my car. "I'll text you later," he says before kissing me and closing my door.

I go to turn on my engine but right as I do, it instantly starts sputtering. "Oh, no. Not now," I groan.

Max turns around and walks back to my car, then opens my door. "Woah, does it always do that?"

"Yeah, sometimes," I sigh.

"Hmm," Max mumbles before he starts walking around the beamer while giving it an intense glance. "Pop the hood."

I do as he asks, and he lifts the hood. After a moment, he closes it and then comes back to my driver side door. He tilts his head and scrunches up his mouth like he is thinking before he says, "I think that you have a mass air flow censor problem. It can keep the car from turning on or it could make it sputter. It's pretty costly to fix. I had to get mine fixed a few months ago. It was a couple hundred."

"Ugh," I groan and slouch down in my driver seat.

More money that I don't have but need to spend because of

this mysterious jackass driver.

"I have an idea," Max says as he reaches for my hands. He pulls me up from the seat and I reluctantly let him. "You need nature."

"Nature?" I repeat as I look at him ponderously.

"Yes, nature," he nods. "You need peace. You said you never go to Townshed. I think you need a day or two away from this city. It will help clear your mind," he smiles. "If you'd like, we can spend a night at my family's house next weekend. I can take you camping out in the backyard... that way you can get the full nature experience," he grins.

"How do you know I've never been camping before?" I smirk.

"You told me that you never left Forest Hill before. You can't get a real camping experience here, no matter how hard you try," he laughs. "My brother and I were planning on turning the house into an Airbnb, but we still have a few things to fix up before we can do it, so the house is empty." He releases my hands and moves his finger from the tip of my ear down to the length of my neck as he pushes my hair back. "It's really peaceful out there. It would be just us... that is only if you want to."

I move my hand on to his and lift it off the back of my neck. I'm not keen on the camping idea but I'm not going to say no to him. I like being with Max and a weekend away might actually do me some good since I have been really stressed recently. I've never camped ever in my life or ever had an interest to, but lately, I've been doing a shit load of new things that I never thought I'd ever do. So, why not add another to the list, right?

"Okay. You got me. I'm in," I grin and reach up to kiss him. We pull back, his hands swallowing my waist.

"I get off work around 4:00 p.m. on Friday. I can pick

you up after and we can head straight there," he says.

I nod my head. "That works. I get off work at 5:00 p.m."

"Great. I can drop you off at the salon today," he says as he looks at my car. "Because I don't think this thing is starting right now."

I grab my purse out of the passenger seat and let him drive me to work.

CHAPTER 11

I was having a hard time sleeping again and it was starting to really get to me, so I texted Michelle to see if she was awake. She called me right away and she picked me up to go to Stoney's to get something to eat. It's 1:00 in the morning and we haven't done this in forever - hang out at the diner this late at night. I think the last time we came here this late was about three months ago. While we are waiting for Luke (our usual waiter) to bring us our burgers, I am telling Michelle about my junkyard adventures.

"I'm so proud of you! I can't believe you've been on your own investigation… You're basically doing the cops job," she shakes her head.

"I know, right? You're going to think I'm crazy, but I did find something," I pull out my phone and show her the picture of the truck from the second junkyard. "Well, possibly. So, when I was at the Junkyard on Coolidge, I found this truck. I passed by a few others before this one, but they were way too fucked up for me to tell what they looked like before," I say as I show her the photo of the blue truck. "It's the only one there that looked similar to what the cameras caught so I tried to get the guy that worked there to tell me who brought it in, but he wouldn't give me the information," I roll my eyes. "His tone got really defensive. I didn't want to tell him about my accident, so I came up with this dumb lie that I was looking for a stolen truck… which wasn't a good idea because he swore that every vehicle there was registered as soon as I brought it up."

"Are you telling me that you think you found the truck that hit you?" she questions.

"I don't know," I shrug my shoulders. "I just think this truck could be a possibility."

Michelle's eyes show concern as she looks at my phone, then to me. "Hmm," she mumbles.

"Say it," I sigh.

"Don't get mad at me. I know you hate when people tell you to calm down, but I really think you need to chill. You just said that there were other trucks there. You found the first one that possibly looks similar… and you think it's the one."

"Well, it's not like it was the very first truck I saw. I did see others when I went to Jucker's junkyard before I went to the one on Coolidge. And I didn't suspect those. Plus, this truck wasn't in the front rows either. They were in the back of the junkyard which means that those trucks probably weren't brought in recently. At least, that's what the guy at the first place told me, anyway. He said that the vehicles that have been in the lot the longest are placed in the back."

"Did I just hear you say you were playing around a junkyard?" Luke interrupts our conversation as he approaches our table with two cheeseburgers on a tray in his hands.

Luke is a skinny pasty skin toned, five-foot seven-inch tall, lanky guy with a sleeve of comic book characters tattooed on his right arm. He's five years older than us and he likes to always remind us of it every time he waits on us. He also likes to question everything we say and do.

"I was *looking* through a junkyard... not that it's any of your business." I roll my eyes as he puts our burgers on the table in front of us.

"Don't tell me you were scavenging around the big one on Coolidge?"

I raise my eyebrows. "Why?"

"That junkyard is shady as shit! You didn't know that?" He laughs.

"No. How would I know that?" I sigh. "What are you talking about?"

"That place is super sketchy. They take in vehicles without titles or registration all the time," he shakes his head and scrunches his lips.

"How would *you* know?" Michelle crosses her arms.

"How long have you two lived here?" he scoffs.

We both exchange annoyed glances. When we don't answer, he mutters, "children," while shaking his head. "So young, so innocent. That junkyard has always been shady. Everyone in Forest knows that. Cops are constantly there. I took my car in last year after it finally died, and I forgot to bring my title with me. The guy was just willing to take my car without it. I obviously went back home and got it before I gave him my car but-"

"Seriously?" I cut his words off. My eyes narrow as I look at Michelle. "That's probably why that guy was all defensive when I started asking him questions! He was so adamant on telling me that all the vehicles and car parts there are registered. I bet the truck that I was asking about is actually stolen or something!" I look at the picture on my phone again, then I look at Michelle. "Or what if this is actually the truck that hit me? You know my instincts are usually right."

"I don't know what Dora the explorer journey you two are on, but that guy straight up lied to you," Luke condescendingly laughs, then walks back to the kitchen.

"Okay, we came here to get your mind off things," Michelle reminds me as she takes the phone out of my hand. "I know you want to find that asshole but if that place is really shady like Luke says, then you should probably stay away from it. You've already done enough searching right now. Why don't you tell me more about Max? How was the carnival? Are you seeing him again?"

As much as I want to keep talking about the truck, I don't argue with her and I go on to tell her about my run in with Nate at the carnival, then about how Max and I's night ended.

"See, things are getting better for you! Look, you already got laid! I can't believe you didn't tell me sooner though!" She squints her eyes at me as she takes a bite of her burger.

"You weren't the first thing on my mind after having sex, Michelle," I laugh. "But okay, you do make a point. I guess things are getting better for me. I don't know... Max is just different from Nate. He was so chill when I told him that Nate was my ex and that he cheated on me. I also told him that I was in a coma when we woke up in the morning and he took that pretty well too. Then when we were both leaving, the beamer started sputtering and I think he could see that I was aggravated because he offered to take me to his family's house this weekend-"

"HIS FAMILY? YOU'RE MEETING HIS PARENTS ALREADY?" Michelle nearly chokes on her burger when she interrupts me.

"No. Not like that," I giggle. "Actually, he told me that his parents died in a car accident a few years ago. The house is empty. I guess he was planning on turning it into an Airbnb with his brother, but they haven't done it yet."

"Holy shit," she gasps again. Her eyes keep getting wider.

"I know, right?" I agree. "Pretty tragic..."

"Yeah, really tragic," she pauses. "Well, you did say yes to him, right? You are going this weekend?"

I nod my head, yes and she squeals. "Max said I need quote on quote nature," I sigh.

"Nature?" She questions me in the same way I questioned Max when he offered. "Ah, so that's why he's the way he is. He's not a city boy."

I bust out laughing. "I was thinking the same thing. But isn't this kind of soon though? I've only been on three dates with him, well four... if you count our lunch date the other day."

"Dude, you already got laid and that was after you went on a lunch date with him. You guys sound like an old married couple already. I don't think it's too soon at all. You should have fun. Things are changing in your life. Just let them change and ride the wave," she says as she makes a wave motion with her right hand.

I scrunch my forehead and chuckle. "I'm starting to hate those quotes you learned."

"You're the one that died on me for a week," she shrugs while smirking. "It's your fault I learned them."

—

After what Luke said to us at the diner, I of course could not sleep when I got home. I was too busy thinking about the junkyard, so I started searching on the internet for information about the place. Unfortunately, the only info that I could find was when the business started which was ten years ago. There are only six customer reviews and there is no website listed or social media for it though. There is only a phone number which I find weird because most businesses, no matter what they are, normally have a website or at least more reviews, especially if they've been in business for so long. I surprisingly didn't see any news reports or articles about the place either. Luke said that cops are constantly there but if that's the case, then I would expect to see something on the internet. Then again, Luke could have been just trying to mess with me too. The only useful information that I did find are the operating hours which are from 8:00 a.m. to 9:00 p.m.

It's only 5:15 a.m. right now and the sun doesn't rise for another hour. On impulse, I put on my sneakers, grab my jacket, and head out my front door and into the parking lot to my car. Just because it stalled yesterday doesn't mean that it won't start today. It has it's good and bad days. I'm hoping today is one of its good days. After a few turns of the key, luckily the ignition finally turns on.

Just a few minutes later, I turn onto Coolidge Street and approach the junkyard. I turn off my headlights as I pull my beamer off the side of the road and into the grass so I can park it next to the fence. I get out of my car, but I leave it running just in case it decides to not turn back on again when I come back out.

For such a supposedly shady place, I'm surprised that there isn't barbed wire over the wooden fence. I've only ever jumped a fence one time in my life and that was in high school for senior skip day. I think it was the same height as the one in front of me but the one in high school was a chain link fence, so I was able to stick my shoes in between the holes when I jumped it. I realize that jumping over this one is going to be a lot trickier. I stick my phone inside of my bra, against my left boob since I'm not prepared for my journey as I chose to wear leggings with no pockets.

Then I try to jump up to reach the top of the fence with my hands, but I poorly fail. I step back to try to take a bit of a running start, but I fail at reaching for it again. There is no way I am going to be able to reach the top of the fence from the ground if I keep jumping, so I get back in my car and pull it closer to the fence. Now, I should be able to reach easier if I jump from the roof of my car.

I climb on top of my roof and take one jump. I am shocked at myself when I finally grab hold of the top of the fence with my hands and I swing my right leg over it. I am straddling the fence in between my legs, and it is extremely uncomfortable. I didn't think about the deep drop into the yard or the fact that there are piles of sharp metal and rusted car parts leaning up against the fence, but now I have no choice but to jump down and try to land away from all of it. I swing my left leg over to the other side and kick off of it with my feet, so I can land as far away from the piles of sharp objects as I can.

However, as soon as my left leg reaches over to the other side, I lose all upper body strength and I fall to the ground a lot faster than I expected I would. My right foot stumbles over the loose parts while my left foot lands onto the dirt grass and I fall on my knees.

I really could've just seriously injured myself or I could have broken my arm again, or maybe even my leg… but I'm glad I'm here. The same adrenaline that came over me after I drove around the curve on Burr Oak is suddenly back. I stand up and turn on the flashlight on my phone and begin to silently walk around while I look for the truck.

I think I slightly sprained my right ankle because it's throbbing when I step on it but it's not enough to stop me. There are only two outdoor lights illuminating the junkyard which makes parts of the lot pretty dark so it's hard for me to remember where the truck is.

It takes me a few minutes to find it, but the moment I do, I rush toward it. I immediately shine my flashlight over the windshield to look for the VIN number, (which I googled where to find it because I had no idea where to look for it before that), and I take a picture of it quickly. Right as I am done and I am checking the photo, I hear a man yell from my right. Out of panic, I start to run back toward the direction of where I jumped over the fence, regardless of the shooting pain in my ankle.

"Keep running and I will release my dog on you!" he yells, and I instantly stop. I'll never be able to outrun a dog and make it all the way to the fence which is still a good ten feet away from me.

Shit, I didn't even really plan on how I was going to jump back over it to get back to my car anyway.

I put my hands up in the air before I slowly turn around. The owner is briskly walking toward me with his rottweiler which is growling and keeping an intense eye on me.

"I'm... I'm sorry," I immediately stutter.

"You again?" he asks in a more annoyed than angry tone in his voice now. He takes a few more steps closer to me, still shining the flashlight at my face. "My boy could've killed you. What are you doing on my property? You're breaking in and trespassing."

"I understand. I'm so-- so sorry," I begin apologizing profusely as I try to block out the light from my eyes with my hand. *I guess he didn't see me take a picture because he hasn't said anything yet.*

He lowers the flashlight. I can see his face slightly enough in the low light. He's holding a more contemplative than annoyed look now. "Why are you here?"

"Uh, I," I hesitate, "I was just looking for a mass air flow censor," I stutter as I remember Max telling me that is what is probably wrong with my car.

"So, you thought breaking in would be the way to get it?"

"I... uh," I stutter. "I don't know. I'm really broke. I can't afford it. I guess... I guess I just, I thought I'd get away with stealing one. I'm so sorry." I keep apologizing since that is all I can really do right now because I think I am either about to go to jail or become this dog's food.

The guy gives me a contemplating look. "Is that really why you were here?"

"I swear," I exhale.

"You weren't looking for a stolen truck again?" He raises his eyebrows.

"Uh... no, I swear! Just look at my car outside. It's barely running. I left it on just in case it died... that's-- that's how desperate I am!"

He steps closer to me which makes me take a step back. His dog is now just about an inch away from me while still holding a low growl. "Don't let me catch you back here. Leave now."

I hesitate for a second because I'm not sure I can move.

"Get the hell out of here! Don't come back!" he repeats, and I immediately unfreeze myself and jog toward the gate which is now open. The man stayed back inside of the yard with his dog as I run out and around to the side of the fence where I left my car.

When I get home, I immediately sit on my couch with my laptop to search the VIN number. Several websites come up in the search results that claim to offer free information, so I click on the first one that is listed. A generated report comes up after I enter the VIN number and I scroll through the make, model, year and all the damages that have been reported on it. I don't see any of the previous owner's information, so I continue to scroll to the bottom where there is a button that requires me to pay for more information. It costs ten dollars. Cringing, I type my credit card number and wait for the rest of the information to come up. *Again, more money that I need to spend when I shouldn't have to thanks to this mysterious asshole.*

The report comes up, but I don't see any of the previous owners listed. It basically gives me the same information that it gave me before I paid. Frustrated, I exit out of the website and then I click on the next few links in my google search. I try three more websites in the list, using the free report tool on each one, but they all give me the same information. None of them have any of the owners listed.

Before I decide to pay for anything else, I search the exact phrase: **websites that will give me the previous owners name on vehicles with only a VIN number.**

Since the first link looks like an advertisement, I click on the second link that is listed in my new search so I can read the reviews. Most are five stars, and a lot of the comments say they were satisfied with the service. The cost for the full report is $37.50. Sighing, I enter my credit card info and hope that it will give me the vehicle's information that I need.

When I click pay, a message appears on the screen that says it will not take my card. I look at the numbers that I entered on the screen, then I compare them to the numbers on my credit card in front of me. They both match perfectly, so I click on the pay option again, but I get the same message.

I had a little over $60.00 left in my checking yesterday. There should be enough money to pay this report after I just paid the other, but I go to check my bank balance anyway. I have only $12.37 in my checking and $20.00 in my savings. I used literally almost all my savings when I enrolled in college the other day and I don't get paid until tomorrow morning, so I have to wait to pay for this report when I get out of work. I'll just have to remember to do it first thing, since Max is going to pick me up to take me to Townshed right when I get home.

As I think about his offer to take me for a weekend of peace, I chuckle out loud. He really *has no idea* how badly I need the weekend away that he offered. I look at the time on my laptop. It's already almost 8:00 a.m. and I work at noon. I didn't get any sleep so I'm going to try to take a two-hour nap before my shift starts. I can't do anything about this truck until tomorrow anyway.

CHAPTER 12

Max's property is huge. It took an hour to get here since the house is all the way at the end of town and we just made it here as the sun is starting to set. Being on the highway made me nervous again, so I decided to just close my eyes on the way. I ended up falling asleep until just after we pulled into a long narrow stone driveway a moment ago. It is in front of a separate garage which is just a few feet away parallel to an incredibly adorable, one-story brick bungalow house.

White windowsills match the front porch which has two white steps, and a burgundy-colored front door. I look out of the passenger window and admire the open land around us. "I didn't know you lived this far into Townshed. It's so open out here," I remark.

"The closest neighbor is a mile away," he says while putting his SUV into park and turning off the engine.

"I've never lived so far away from people," I say as I continue to admire the football field sized backyard which lines into the woods.

Growing up in Forest, I have only lived in apartments, and they never looked anything remotely like this. My parents were never able to afford rent for anything bigger than an apartment, so I have always lived right next to people. Seeing a house like this is a little weird to me. We get out of the truck, and I follow Max the few feet across the front yard from the driveway and into the front door of the house. He holds out his arm, allowing me to walk in first when he opens the door.

I am in awe when I step right into a very cozy living room with cabin like walls, even though the outside doesn't resemble a cabin one bit. To the left of the doorway, a long tan leather sofa sits in front of a fireplace. A glass coffee table with a dolphin shape sculpture for the base divides them and right behind the living room is the kitchen which is decorated with white cabinets and granite countertops. A small bar with three high stools sitting beneath it, divides the living room and kitchen. For a usually empty house, I am shocked at how clean and tidy it is.

"I thought this house was empty... It looks like it was just cleaned," I remark.

"Oh, that's because I came here and cleaned up yesterday after work. I needed to turn on the water and electric for the weekend for us anyway," he shrugs.

"Wow," I mumble as that's all I can say because I feel kind of weird, but also... happy that he went through so much trouble for me.

Max leads me through the living room, and we go through a white door to the left of the kitchen. "And here is where we will be staying," he says as we walk into a master bedroom. It has a queen size bed which is dressed in red satin sheets and there are two dressers beside it. A flat screen television is mounted on the wall in front of the bed. My eyes light up when I take a few more steps into the room and see a bathroom with a double sink vanity set and a deep bathtub with frameless shower doors inside.

"I knew you'd like it," he says.

"You noticed my eyes didn't you," I giggle.

"I always take notice of your eyes," he smiles.

Every time Max flirts with me, I feel a chill down my spine. He leans into me, his hands gripping around my waist, and I reach up on my toes to kiss him. He leans in closer, my lips falling into his. I love the feeling of his hands when they move up and down my body gently. He picks me up and I lock my feet around his hips.

In between kisses all over my body, he carries me out of the bathroom and on top of the satin sheets on the bed.

—

The sounds of the birds chirping woke me up right as the sun started rising. Max, on the other hand, snored right through them. I helped him set up a tent at the edge of the backyard just a few feet into the woods last night and I surprisingly enjoyed sleeping outside. I wasn't scared of being out there because I was able to see the house from where we were, so it wasn't like we were deep into the woods. I was also able to go use the bathroom inside whenever I needed because there was no way that I was going to go out there. Sleeping in the tent wasn't *that* uncomfortable, although a mattress definitely feels better in my opinion... but overall, just being out in nature and away from the city really was a good experience for me. I didn't know that I would actually enjoy it as much as I did. I fell asleep in Max's arms pretty quickly and I didn't wake up once throughout the night... that's how relaxed I felt.

Even though I am awake at the crack of dawn and running on only five hours of sleep, I don't feel tired. I was going to wake up Max just now but instead, I decided to let him keep sleeping and I went back inside the house to surprise him with breakfast. We brought a cooler with some sandwich meats, bread, eggs, bacon, a bottle of wine, and two steak dinners with vegetables and potatoes with us. Max said he wanted to cook a nice dinner for me tonight which I'm really excited for because I've never had a guy cook for me ever. The only person that I'm used to cooking for me is my mother.

The bacon is almost done cooking on the stove, and I am beginning to put the eggs on the pan when Max opens the slider door. "You're up early," he says.

"The birds woke me up," I answer as I whip the eggs on the pan.

"Figured." He hugs me around my waist from behind and kisses me on the cheek. "Oh, breakfast! Thank you, babe," he says before he starts to brew a pot of coffee beside me. I like how we are moving in sync throughout the kitchen.

I could get used to this.

The sun is fully risen now, and we can still hear the birds chirping when we take our plates outside to eat at the table on the porch.

"So besides being awoken by the birds, how did you like sleeping outside? You can be honest too Miss City girl," he playfully teases.

"Woah! No one has ever called me a city girl," I laugh. "I actually enjoyed camping. I mean, a mattress would've made it a little more comfortable, but I guess your arms were good enough." I give him a flirtatious smirk and he flexes his arms as he looks down at his biceps.

"Weighted blankets. So, I think I know the answer but I'm going to ask anyway," he pauses, "Have you ever been hiking?"

I say nothing and just press my lips into a smile before I

take a bite of my eggs.

He laughs, "that's what I thought."

"Is that why you told me to bring a pair of boots?" I ask.

"I was trying to keep it a surprise, but I wanted to make sure you're at least a bit prepared," he says as he finishes the last bite of his eggs. He eats way quicker than me since he is about a hundred pounds more than me.

"Well, I'm going to go gather some things from the basement then. I would love for you to keep those tight leggings on all day, but I think you might want to wear something more covering. The deeper we go into the woods; mosquitos are going to eat you alive through those."

"I'll go change while you get things ready," I say as I finish the last few bites of my eggs.

I go into the room and dress accordingly while Max gets whatever we need. At first, I was hesitant on the whole nature idea but I'm really glad I'm here. I changed into a pair of jeans but still kept my long sleeve shirt on and added a light hoodie over it before going to find Max.

The basement door is open, and I can hear him shuffling through things downstairs, so I go down to see what he's getting. I find him hunched over an opened cardboard box next to a couple other piles of boxes in the back of the basement. He's pulling items out and setting them on the table nearby. He turns toward me when he hears me come down the steps.

"Alright, I got us some bug spray, water bottles, a compass... even though I know these woods like the back of my hand, it's still always good to have, first aid kit, bear mace, and-"

"Woah! Hold on," I cut his words off. "Bear what?"

He starts chuckling, "you do know that animals live in

the woods, right?"

"Uh, yes," I give him a sarcastic look. "But uh, do you encounter bears often?"

"Well, we didn't encounter any last night," he shrugs.

"True," I mumble but I keep a pensive look on my face.

"We'll be fine," Max assures me with a grin. He finishes putting the items in two bags. He hands me one, then grabs the other one and we go back up the steps to begin our hike.

—

The hike wasn't bad at all. Beside the fact that I was slightly on edge every time I heard a twig snap because I immediately started thinking that a bear was going to come up and maul us to death, the hike was nice and peaceful. Other than my slight paranoia, I think I stayed overall calm the whole time.

We ended up being out in the woods for two hours, but I didn't even realize it until we got back to the house. We were both starving so I made us two ham and cheese sandwiches and we just sat across from each other at the table on the patio in the backyard to eat them.

When I sit down, I put my phone on the table and the name *Nate* appears on my screen as it rings. *I bet he's trying to call me now because he saw me with Max the other day. Typical.* Besides running into him at the carnival, the last time he reached out to me on his own was a month before my accident happened. I think I just showed visible aggravation in my face because Max is looking at me oddly.

"You alright?" he asks.

"Uh, yeah," I say as I hit deny on the call. "How is the sandwich?"

"It's perfect," he smiles, and my phone goes off again but this time it's my alarm.

"Birth control," I sigh. "I'll be right back."

"Oh, yeah... please, go take that!" Max says in a joking, but serious manner and it makes me shyly laugh.

After I take my pill out of my purse in the bathroom, I look at myself in the mirror. I brush my hands through my bangs which reveals the scar on my forehead, and I remember that I didn't pay for the report on the truck yesterday after work. I completely forgot once I got home because I had to pack to come here, and then Max picked me up shortly after. Now, I have the slight urge to pay for it after I'm done eating my lunch, but I'll just wait until I get back home instead.

As badly as I want to know whose truck that is, I need to remember that I'm here to relax. I'm here to enjoy my time with Max. Another day of not finding out who this person is won't make any difference. I know if I look at the report now, then whether I find good or bad information, it won't leave my mind until I can do something about it and I don't want that to happen. I came here to get my mind off everything.

When I walk back outside, Max has already eaten half of his food as I expected he would by now. "No babies here today," I smirk as I sit back down. I look around outside and admire the open land as I keep eating my sandwich.

There's a very old, rusted swing set just a few feet away from us, closest to the house but besides that, the rest of the yard is wide open. The morning fog is starting to dissipate which is opening the land in view.

"I know we came here to take your mind off things babe, but how are you feeling now?" he asks. "How's your head doing?"

"I'm okay," I nod. "It's not hurting right now. This has been a great distraction. I'm really happy you took me here." I look toward the woods. "It's peaceful out here."

"Good, that was my goal," he smiles. "I was thinking, I might be able to get someone to fix your car for cheap. Did the sputtering start after your accident?"

"No, I wasn't driving the beamer when it happened," I answer. "I was driving my little scion, but it got totaled. The beamer is my dad's car. He's just letting me use it until I can afford a new one," I say before I take a bite of my sandwich and swallow. "I miss my scion though. It was the cutest car ever. It was my first car. I only had it for a little over a year. I just wish that the cops found the driver that hit me," I mumble in annoyance as I think about my totaled car.

"What do you mean?" he looks at me with a puzzled face and I realize that I never told him that my accident was a hit and run yet.

"The person that crashed into me drove away and the cops never found them," I sigh.

"So, it was a hit and run?" he questions.

"Yeah," I nod. "The cops ended up closing my case last week and well uh, you might think I'm crazy..." I hesitate before continuing to tell him about my own investigation. I don't want to sound like I'm a paranoid person, but I also don't want to not tell him about what's been going on with me. I don't think that Max will judge me and I'm hoping that my instincts are right. "I've been looking for the person that hit me," I sigh.

The look of concern in Max's face turns into puzzlement. "What do you mean? How have you been doing that?"

"Well, when the police closed the case, it infuriated me,

so I decided to go back to the spot of my accident. Long story short, I ended up going to every house around the area to ask the residents if they saw anything the night I got hit. A lady gave me a description of a truck that was speeding by around that time so, I've been going off what she told me," I pause as I think about almost getting attacked by the dog at the junkyard. "I think I found a truck that matches her description at one of the junkyards in Forest, but I don't know, I could be wrong. I have the VIN number. I planned on looking it up when I got back home."

I look at Max who is now staring at me with narrowed eyes. I don't feel like I should tell him that I got detained at the police station or how exactly I got the VIN number, so I'll just leave it at that. He doesn't look like he's judging me, like I hoped he wouldn't, but I don't want to overwhelm him with more. If I do, he might start to worry that I'm actually going crazy because honestly, I'm starting to question that myself lately... especially after hearing what I just said to him out loud. "I know. It sounds insane," I sigh. "But I just really want this person to get caught. They literally almost killed me and honestly... it's hard to get over."

After a moment, his face loosens and looks right in my eyes. "You're incredible, you know that?" I am in shock at his response. I wasn't sure what it was going to be, but I didn't think he'd call me incredible. "Uh, thanks..." I say with confusion.

He scooches his chair closer to me and reaches for my hand. "I'm serious, Jen. I can't believe you've been going through so much. You're really strong for doing all that," he says before kissing me on the lips.

His compliment fills my heart with ease. I don't know

why I was nervous to tell Max this. I feel better that I told him. I like how supportive and calm he is, especially now. It's a good balance as my emotions have been everywhere these past few weeks.

"So, you really don't think I'm crazy for trying to find this person?" I question.
Max shakes his head and smiles as he rubs the back of my thumb with his. "I think it just means you're very determined. And, I don't blame you for looking for the person at all." He stands up. "I forgot to stop at the store on the way here to get some spices for our dinner tonight. Do you want to come with, or do you want to stay here and relax? It should take me about half an hour."

"I'll stay because I'm dying to shower," I grin as I look myself up and down.

"Me too," he laughs as he starts walking in the house, "but I'm just going to change into a hoodie before I go."

A minute later, he comes back out from the bedroom as I am walking in from the porch with our empty plates. "Text me if you need anything," he says before kissing me, and heading out the front door.

After he left, I took a quick shower, then I dressed into my leggings and a new fitted dark blue long-sleeve V-neck. We didn't put the hiking gear away yet, so I decide to take them back down to the basement to clean up. It takes me two trips because I forget one of the bags upstairs.

When I am finished putting the last bag in the corner of the basement by the window, I take a minute to look around. I'm not being nosey but I'm really just admiring the place. It's a spacious basement and it has a small bathroom in the left corner near the laundry machines. I go in curiously to look when I stop to view my reflection in the mirror.

My hair is in desperate need of brushing now that it is out of its messy bun, that I had put it into when I showered. I didn't bring any shampoo to wash it, so I didn't want to get it wet. There are already a few knots in it. I forgot to bring my hairbrush too, so I open the cabinet under the sink to see if there is one here. Inside is a basket with toilet paper and a couple of old shampoo bottles, but I don't see any hairbrushes. At least it didn't hurt to look. I'll have to find one upstairs or keep the messy bun look until I go back home. I leave the bathroom and go back up the steps to wait for Max in the living room but when I go to turn the doorknob to leave the basement, it won't open. I try again with more strength, but it won't budge.

"There's no way I just locked myself in here," I mumble. I try to pull the doorknob with both hands three more times, but it still doesn't open. I know the door opens in toward the kitchen, so I try to push on it in hopes that I can maybe force it enough for the lock to break, but it doesn't work either. I stop pushing it after a few times when I realize that I have my cell phone in the waistband of my legging.

I'll just call Max and tell him to come unlock the door when he gets back rather than try to keep breaking it open. He should be back soon anyway. After I click on his name in my contacts, I wait for it to start ringing but it goes straight to voicemail. I assume that he probably forgot to charge it. He said it should take him half an hour to get to the store and he left about twenty minutes ago so he should be back soon.

But *what am I going to do until then? Sit here helplessly?* There has got to be a way that I can get myself out of here on my own without damaging his property before he comes back. I don't want to seem like such a damsel in distress because I feel like I already do.

I take a moment to think and look around the basement when I spot the window. It's about a foot higher than me but if I stand on something, I can get it open and I think I'm small enough to crawl out of it. I know I left the back door unlocked so if I get out, I can just go walk around to the back yard and go into the house through there. Then, Max won't have to come back and find me sitting helplessly down here.

I go over to where the step ladder is wedged in between one of the stacked boxes in the back of the basement. I set my phone down on one of the boxes, while I move some of the others out of my way to reach the ladder. After I drag it over and climb up, I go to open the window, but it doesn't work. It doesn't budge at all. After a few more times of trying, I give up and sit down on the top step of the ladder.

Just when I am beginning to think that I'm really going to have to wait here helplessly until Max comes back, I hear his SUV pulling into the driveway. I stand back up to look out the window to see that the garage door is pulled up. He must've parked inside this time because the door wasn't left open before.

My assumptions are right as seconds later, he walks out of the garage and starts to pull the door down to close it.

"MAX!" I slam my palms against the window, and I see him turn his head over towards the house. I didn't think he'd hear me from here but I'm glad he did. I guess I could have waited for him to get into the house before calling out like a dramatic person but too late now. At least he knows I'm down here. I climb back down the ladder without putting it away and I head for the basement door.

Just as I am reaching the top of the steps, I see the

doorknob turn. "I must've locked myself in here," I go to say but my words are cut short when I realize that it isn't Max at the door. I have no time to move or turn around before I catch a glimpse of a man's tattooed hands coming right at me. In the next few seconds, I'm falling backward down the stairs and just like when my accident happened, I don't have any time to react to it.

CHAPTER 13

It feels like I'm waking up from my coma all over again but this time, I'm not in the hospital and it hasn't been a week. I think I got knocked out during my fall down the stairs, but it had to have been for only for a couple minutes because this time I don't remember being in a white room. I last remember seeing the man by the door and then getting pushed by him. I know that I tried to break my fall with my hands when I tumbled down the stairs because I didn't want my head to get hurt… but I clearly didn't do a good enough job of blocking it because I'm tied up to the water heater's pipe and I don't remember it happening.

I'm sitting up on the floor across from the stacks of boxes next to the washer and dryer and my hands are tied by thick rope to the pipe in front of me. As I begin to move my head, a sharp pain runs through the nape of my neck and down into my shoulder blades. The room is slightly spinning and I'm on the edge of nausea. My head is throbbing so terribly that I can hear ringing in both of my ears.

Trying not to panic, I search the room with my eyes when I remember putting my phone on top of one of the boxes before I went to move the step ladder over to the window earlier. The rope is tied tightly around my wrists, but I try to pull away from the pipe with all my strength anyway. But I don't have enough strength because the rope doesn't loosen any bit.

I even place my foot against the washer to the left of me, so I can use it for leverage, while I keep trying to pull away but that doesn't work either. I am sitting down but I think I can wiggle the rope up the pipe just enough to allow me to stand up on my feet. I stand up, slightly hunched over as I pull my wrists up and down the pipe to loosen it a few times. The rope is tied tightly which makes my wrists burn with every tug, but I've managed to loosen it enough to allow some wiggle room to shimmy it up and down the pipe an inch or two. Now I am standing upright so I can look toward the boxes for my cell phone.

A sigh of relief washes over me when I see it. The only way that I'll only be able to reach it from here, is if I make the boxes fall over so my phone can fall off. I need it to fall close enough toward me so I can at least be able to grab it with my feet. I can't reach the boxes while I'm standing, so I sit back down on the floor.

Moving the rope all the way down the pipe to the base of the heater with me, I shimmy myself down on to the floor so I can lay on my left side. I need to extend my legs as close as I can get them to the boxes. Every inch of the muscles in my limbs feel like they are being pulled apart when I stretch my body out when I kick... and *it fucking hurts,* but I'm not going to quit. I keep kicking rapidly at the boxes with my right foot while using my left foot for leverage against the ground. With every kick, my body aches even more but I'm not going to allow the pain to stop me.

After about ten or so more kicks, my phone finally falls to the ground, but it doesn't fall in front of me by my feet where I wanted it to. Instead, it fell to the right just a few inches away from my bare feet. I'm just barely able to touch it with my toes when I kickout and I manage to grip it just slightly enough to pull it back toward me with my foot.

Fumbling once I have the phone in my hand, I start to dial 911 but I hear a loud thud above me, and it startles me so bad that I drop it. Between my trembling hands and my throbbing headache, I am trying to remain calm but *fuck, it's difficult.*

I'm scrambling on the floor to pick my phone back up when I see the basement door open. I quickly slide my phone behind the washer next to me just in time before I see the man that pushed me come through the doorway. He leaves the door open and starts walking down the staircase, stopping only a couple steps down. He's keeping his head low and his ball cap is forward so I can't really see his face.

"Are you okay?" he asks in such a low voice that I can barely hear him.

Is he really asking me that right now?

"Are you okay?" he repeats a little louder after I don't answer.

"*Am I okay?*" I widen my eyes. "What the fuck do you think?" I shout in a perplexed and shaken voice. "Who the fuck are you?"

He ignores my question and instead asks in the same low tone, "are you hurt?"

"AM I HURT?" My voice grows louder, along with my eyes. *Whoever this man is, he has lost his damn mind.* "YES, I'M FUCKING HURT. WHAT IS GOING ON? WHO ARE YOU?" I demand but he doesn't answer me. "MAX! MAX!"

As soon as I start calling out for Max, the man immediately rushes back up the steps and closes the door shut behind him. *Shit! What if he didn't know Max was here too? Did I just put him in danger? Or does Max know he's here? Where is he anyway? I swear I saw him coming out of the garage... but where the hell is he now?*

I stand back up to step closer to the washer so I can try to reach behind it for my phone with my leg. When I don't feel it with my toes, I kick the washer out just an inch more so I can see behind it better and when I do, I feel like crying. I guess since I was panicking, I shoved it with so much force that it got wedged all the way behind the dryer and in between the wall. I threw it too far to be able to reach it with my leg from where I'm at.

Fuck. Fuck. Fuck. Panic is setting in. *This isn't good.* A lump of fear is emerging inside of my stomach. The room is spinning and the nausea that was starting to settle is coming back again. I need to breathe but I think I forgot how because it's becoming extremely difficult to get air. I'm hyperventilating and my face is beginning to tingle while my chest is feeling tight. This is the beginning feelings of a panic attack and it's not the time for one right now. *I need air... I need out of here.*

I have no idea who that guy is or what his intentions are with me, but I don't want to find out. I close my eyes to take a moment to control myself. Freaking out right now isn't going to help me. The only way I'm going to be able to reach my phone again, is if I find something to use to somehow pull it toward me.

When I was kicking at the boxes before, a box fell off the top and some string lights, along with a couple ornament balls spilled out near where my phone had fallen. There is nothing else in my reach besides the decorations, so I'll have to make use of them.

After dragging my hands back down to the base of the

pipe again to sit back down, I slump down on my side like I had before. The flesh on my forearms and my wrist burns with every tug and stretch, but the pain is not going to stop me from reaching those lights. *Nothing is going to stop me from fighting my way out of here.*

I scrunch my toes into the bottom of the top of my feet as I start to kick toward the lights. After just two tries, I'm able to grab them and pull the lights back toward my body in the same way as I got my phone. Doing my best with my tied-up hands, I stand back up on to my feet. Then I hold one end of the lights while I throw the other behind the washer toward my phone. After several tosses, I realize that it's not doing me any good. The end of the lights only graze over my phone. I think my phone is too heavy to be able to pull it... unless I can somehow catch it with the lights instead.

I quickly tie the string of lights into a small but big enough circle so that my phone could fit through it, before I try to toss it behind the washer. I don't really have the confidence that this will work but I know that I have to at least try. It's the only thing I can think to do right now. I rather try something then just wait here like a sitting duck.

After way too many tosses, I give up and throw the lights back toward the boxes on the floor. They brush up against one of the ornament balls when they land which makes it roll closer to me. Out of sheer hope and frustration, I take it and toss it behind the washer, hoping the ball will do something but just like the Christmas lights, it didn't help. The tingly feeling in my cheeks is coming back. "MAX!!! MAX!!!" I'm screaming his name regardless of what I feel right now. "HELP! SOMEONE! HELP!"

I don't know what else to do anymore but just keep calling out for help.

—

I think about twenty minutes passed by when I finally stopped yelling. I was so loud and persistent that I even shocked myself. My throat is sore now and I feel dehydrated which isn't helping my nausea. Yelling also didn't help the massive headache that I've had either, but I just couldn't help myself. I tried pulling away from the pipe so many times that the skin on my wrists and the part of my forearms that are tied to it is starting to bleed. I'm getting dizzier and weaker by the minute.

If only I didn't push my phone back so far behind the damn laundry machines. I'm so mad at myself for doing that but I know that I can't give up. Suddenly, I hear a loud thud above me. It sounded like it was the front door slamming shut. I'm starting to hear distant voices upstairs, but I can't make out the words clearly. I can't tell whose voice it is, so I start yelling again. "HELP! HELP!"

With every yell, my throat gets more horse, and my head continues to throb. I desperately need water, *but I don't care.* I keep yelling as loud as I can until a flood of light from the kitchen shines through the doorway when the basement door flings open. The same man that pushed me is rushing down the staircase. When he gets to the last step, he stands there silently while keeping his head low.

Seconds later, I hear more footsteps, so I direct my attention to the top of the staircase, and I see Max rushing down them. He stops just a few steps away from the other guy as soon as he sees me. "Holy, shit," he gasps, then mumbles something too low for me to understand.

"I-I-I can't hear you," I stutter. "W-what's going on? Why am I tied up?" A page of questions is running through my mind right now, but I can't get them all out at once. Max isn't fighting the guy. He isn't pushing past him. He's just staring at me with his mouth dropped open.

"I'm... I'm so sorry," he says, voice low and shaky. He's looking at me with a look I've never seen on him. "I didn't mean for this to happen. I didn't know what else to do. I didn't know..."

"What are you talking about? What's going on?" I glare at him, then I look at the other guy.

"This-- this is my brother, Phil," Max says quietly.

"I'm sorry," I hear Phil mutter but he's still keeping his head low.

"Sorry for fucking pushing me down the stairs?" I shout in disbelief.

"It was an accident," he mutters, still avoiding eye contact with me by looking down at his feet.

"AN ACCIDENT? PUSHING ME WASN'T A FUCKING ACCIDENT YOU ASS! WAS TYING ME UP TO THIS PIPE AN ACCIDENT TOO?" I shout.

Phil doesn't answer. He doesn't even pick his head up to look at me. I look at Max because I am expecting him to come help me but he's just staring down at Phil and shaking his head. His body language is stiff as a board and it's scaring me.

"Max, what is going on?" I desperately plead.

He takes a deep breath before he looks at me and says, "Jen. Phil was the one who crashed into you."

I just saw his lips move and I heard the words, but I don't want to understand them. *This isn't possible... This can't be possible right now...*

"No, no, no," I shake my head in disbelief. I feel like I'm about to hyperventilate. I'm fighting back tears and the urge to throw up everywhere. "What? Why? Did- did you guys' plan this? I don't understand... Max, what the fuck?"

"I didn't know that Phil was going to do this to you!" Max says urgently. His face is showing visible confusion and frustration as he looks at Phil, who still hasn't moved. The fact that Phil is still just standing there with his head down is infuriating.

"You almost killed me! You asshole! You're a piece of fucking shit!" I shout at him, but it doesn't make him show me his face. I have been longing to see the person who sent me into my coma, but I didn't know what I would do when, or, if I ever met them. I know that I wanted whoever it was to get caught or at least face some type of consequence for what he or she did to me. Whether it would be jail time, probation, or if it was money for all the damages that occurred, and that I still have to pay for... really anything would have made me happy.

But I didn't ever plan to actually see the person in front of me and now that I do, I feel all the nerves inside of my body fill with anger and I have the greatest urge to tackle him. "Why did you push me? Why am I tied up!?" I demand to the both of them.

"I'm untying her man! This is ridiculous!" Max goes to step down the stairs, but Phil turns and pushes him back up the steps instantly. He's about an inch taller than Max and visibly stronger so Phil's push made Max stumble back, but he was able to steady himself by holding the railing.

"No, you're not, man!" Phil grunts and I can see Max roll his eyes. If he really wants to come untie me... he's not trying that hard.

"Jen," Max looks over at me. "I didn't know that it was you he crashed into, I swear! I didn't plan to meet you. I didn't plan for any of this to happen," he pauses to look at Phil with a displeasing expression, "I saw your text earlier so I called Phil when I shouldn't have-"

"My text? What text?" I interrupt him as I press my eyebrows together.

"The text from whoever sent you a picture of the truck on camera. You left your phone on the table while you went to go get your birth control and I got curious when I saw that Nate texted you, so I checked it," he sighs. "I didn't know it was Phil who hit you until I called him, and he told me-"

"Man! Shut up!" Phil shouts.

"I'm untying her, man," Max shouts back as he starts to step down the staircase past Phil, but he doesn't get far because Phil stops him again.

"NO!" He forcefully pushes Max back up the steps and this time, Max falls back just barely catching his balance on the steps when he lands.

Phil throws his head back in aggravation which makes his ball cap fall off and for the first time, I can see his face. He looks remarkably just like Max. He has a buzzcut like him, except there is just a bit more hair on the top of his head. Unlike Max though, Phil has more facial hair in his goatee and no mustache.

As I look at them, I'm starting to think that I might not have seen Max pulling the garage door down. I thought I saw him but now that I am looking at them, I think it was Phil that I saw. They are both wearing jeans and a hoodie, but Phil is wearing a dark grey one. Max is wearing a dark blue one. I might've just mistaken Phil for Max when I saw him pulling the garage door down.

Suddenly, my thoughts break when we hear the low tone of my ringer from my cell phone behind the washer and Phil comes racing toward me. When he realizes that the sound is coming from behind the laundry machines, he quickly pushes it out and reaches back to get my phone. He picks it up, then quickly rushes past me and over to Max. "It's someone named Michelle. Who is that?" he asks as he looks at me then at Max.

"Uh, her friend," Max answers.

"You should let me answer it!" I quickly say when I look at Max. "She knows I'm with you. If I don't answer her, you know she's going to keep calling me," I try to persuade them quickly before she hangs up. "Max, you know how she is. If I don't answer her, she's going to keep calling and eventually raise hell."

Max ponders what I said for a second before he nods to Phil and tells him to answer it. Phil gives him a discerning look but still accepts the call and puts it on speaker. He nods at me to answer.

"Uh, hello," I try to say in a calm tone.

"Hey! How is everything going there?" Michelle whispers. "I'm hiding in the dressing room at work. You never answered my text this morning, so I called to check on you really quick."

"Uh, it's good. It's going great." I clear my throat. It's almost impossible for me to keep my voice from sounding shaky.

"Are you sure? Are you okay? Am I on speaker? You sound kind of far away." Her voice turns concerned and less of a whisper.

I hesitate for just a second before I bravely yell, "HELP! CALL 911!"

EVERYTHING LED ME TO YOU

As soon as I open my mouth, Phil quickly ends the call. I think I took him off guard because he nearly dropped the phone out of his hand in panic as soon as I raised my voice.

"We need to talk, now," he mutters to Max as he grabs him by the forearm and turns him around, then starts pushing him up the stairs.

"Wait! Don't leave me here! Max! Seriously?!" I breathlessly gasp but Phil is already forcing him through the doorway. The basement door closes behind them and once again, I am alone and still tied up to this fucking water heater.

CHAPTER 14

Max

"Why did you do that? You could've really hurt her!" I shout as I push Phil by his shoulders. "What the fuck is wrong with you? I didn't call you here to kidnap and tie her up like a hostage! You've fucking lost it, man!"

"Dude, I didn't intend for that to happen. When she was opening the door, she freaked out and lunged toward me. I went to stop her, but she fell backward, man!" Phil grunts as he kneels down to look under the kitchen sink.

He's looking for the whiskey, I know it. I pull him up by the back of his shirt, but he pushes me back. "Bro, she said you pushed her down the stairs!" Just as I begin yelling at him, Jen's phone rings in Phil's pocket. He quickly pulls it out to hit ignore when he sees that it's Michelle calling again.

"I didn't! She freaked out and fell back, man, I swear," he huffs. "I wouldn't have hurt her on purpose," he's insisting as he grabs the bottle under the sink.

"Dude, you made her pass out! She was already in a fucking coma because of you! Why the hell did you even tie her up like that?"

"Because I panicked! I can't let her keep investigating! I can't go down for this shit! I'm already on probation!"

"That didn't mean that you had to tie her to a pipe like a hostage!" I shout. "We could've played this out some other way. I could've talked to her! I could have explained everything. I didn't call you to come here! I called you because I had questions! How did you get here anyway? I thought you were at work."

"I took an uber from work. I wasn't going to sit in our apartment while you play house with this girl," Phil grumbles before taking a swig of the whiskey.

"Dude, your fucking losing your mind. I'm going to untie her." I begin to go toward the basement door but Phil steps right in front of me, acting as a barricade between me and the basement.

"NO! You're not untying her! You realize that she could have found the truck here, right? She has footage of it!"

"She didn't see the truck! I made sure I took her the other way when we went hiking this morning," I argue.

"YOU WENT HIKING?" His voice raises along with his eyes. "THE TRUCK IS RIGHT OUT THERE, MAN!"

"I'm not an idiot! I went the opposite way. There was no way she was going to just stumble upon it on her own. She was terrified of the woods. I was with her every minute we were out there," I shake my head. "I also had no idea that you crashed into her. You told me you hit a tree."

"I did hit a tree," he mumbles.

"Yeah, you also failed to tell me that you crashed into another car and sent a person into a coma for a whole fucking week."

Phil rolls his eyes. "It doesn't matter now. Jen has FOOTAGE of that night," he emphasizes as he pulls her phone back out of his pocket. When he does, Michelle calls again, and he hits the ignore button immediately. Only seconds later it rings once more, and Phil's eyes glare right at it.

"It's this bitch again. She keeps calling. I'm turning this

shit off," he says as he holds down the power button to shut the phone off. "Fuck, do you think she heard her yell for help? What if she called the cops? They could be on the way here already!"

I shake my head as I think about it. "No, I doubt that. I never gave Jen this address so Michelle shouldn't have it either. I don't think we need to worry about it, bro. Just calm down, man. We need to think. You made this situation worse than it should be!"

Phil is pacing in small steps right in front of the basement door, still making sure to block me. I can tell that he's seriously freaking out right now which is making me freak out myself. Jen is tied up because of me. If I didn't call Phil, then she wouldn't be down there right now... *but now I'm stuck.* There's no way I'm getting past him while he keeps blocking the door. He's regularly a walking asshole on a sober day. When he's drunk, it's five times worse and he's already chugged almost half the bottle.

"Hell, you knew this girl was in a fucking car accident! How did you not put two and two together?" he asks before he takes another swig.

"Because she never told me that it was a hit and run until today, man! How would I have put those two things together?" I shake my head at him. "You realize that you told me you hit a tree, right? Even if Jen told me that the accident was a hit and run, before we came here, I still would not have realized it was you! I only figured it out because I was snooping on her phone and saw my truck!"

"It doesn't matter now," Phil says as he gives me an annoyingly critical look like he always does. "You should have never even come here. You know the trucks here! You shouldn't be bringing anyone by it!"

"Okay, but I didn't know that she was playing Nancy Drew and was looking for the damn thing." I slam my hand on the kitchen counter. "Just like I didn't know that you crashed into anybody, let alone that it was her, or the fact that you fucking sent her into a coma, man!" My voice is raising with every word, and I can feel my face growing hot. I haven't felt this amount of rage in a year. "You really fucked this shit up. I wouldn't have let you put my truck out here if I knew the truth."

Phil ignores my comments and continues pacing in front of the basement door while he smacks his forehead with his palm repeatedly. "We need to get the truck out of here in case someone comes looking. I can't go down for this shit. I'm already on probation."

"Well, what do you want to do? Drive it into a lake?" I mumble as I start pacing back and forth too. "I bet it won't even start again."

Suddenly, I feel like a brick hits me in the face and I quickly realize it was Phil's fist. He just punched me in my right temple.

"Snap out of it, man!" he grunts. "I don't need your sarcasm shit today!"

Phil's right but at this point I'm over everything. I knew it was probably too early for me to start dating again but Jen was just so... different. I felt such a strong connection to her. She is so beautiful too. I just couldn't help myself... but I should've known better though. I have always believed that I am destined to be unhappy for the rest of my life after my parents died and no matter how hard I try to prove that theory wrong, I fail every time.

"What else did Jen tell you?" My thoughts shift when I hear Phil speak.

"I already told you, bro," I sigh. "She just told me

that she found a truck in some junkyard, and she was planning on searching the VIN number of it when she got back home. She didn't even tell me that she had footage of my truck, and I didn't want to ask her about it because then she would've known that I went through her phone," I pause, "and like I already told you, the cops stopped the investigation. They are not even looking for my truck anymore. According to what Jen told me, she has been the only one looking for it. I really think you need to calm down."

"Okay, but then who sent the picture of the security footage to her phone then? They must know something," he scoffs.

Someone who lived in a house on that street, but I'm not going to tell you that. That will only make things worse if I tell him, so I just shrug my shoulders.

After a moment of pacing, Phil looks at me and sighs. "Alright, I'm sorry, man. I get it. You didn't mean for this to happen."

"Yeah, well if you told me the truth about what really happened that night, then I don't know… maybe, I would've figured it out sooner." I roll my eyes. "Shit, man. I thought I'd have a nice time with her here," I groan. My heart aches as I hear Jen cry below us. She's been doing it this whole time, but I've been focused on Phil. I don't like hearing her cry but now I really don't know what to do. With every minute passing of her down there, I know this whole situation is getting worse, but I don't know how to stop it.

Phil is keeping a firm guard in front of the basement door with his whiskey bottle in hand still. Even if I try to push past him, it will do me no good. He's already swung at me once. The drunker he gets, the worse he becomes. "I was really starting to like her," I mutter in aggravation as I begin to pace small circles.

After another gulp, Phil mumbles, "I know. You took her here... The last girl you took here was Monica."

I shiver when he says her name. *I don't like hearing it anymore.*

"I don't mean to be so hard on you, man. I know her deaths been rough on you," he says before taking another swig from the bottle.

"Well, what's your plan now, genius?" I ask as I cross my arms at my torso.

"Why don't you go find this Michelle girl and stop her from going to the cops. She's probably telling them about you right now?" He gives me a sarcastic look.

"About me?" I stare at him in confusion. "What the hell would she tell them about me?"

"Bro, she heard her best friend yelling the words; call 911 while she's with YOU. I bet she's telling the cops that you are the one that has her in danger. If she doesn't know where this house is, then I'm sure that she's going to figure it out sooner or later! Why don't you go drive by our apartment first? See if there's any cop cars around or something," he lets out a loud aggravating sigh. "I don't know man but none of this is good. You got to go stop that bitch before she makes things worse."

Although Phil is getting more intoxicated by the minute, he still makes a point. Michelle has no idea that Phil is here, and she barely knows me. She had to have heard Jen call for help. Michelle's really protective over Jen in general and she was suspicious of me already since I have no social media. *Great. Once again, like my whole childhood and teenage life, I'm getting fucked over because of Phil.*

"What the fuck do you want me to do if I find her?" I groan.

"I don't know. Figure it out. I'm not the only one on the line here, man," Phil says and at the same time, Jen lets out a loud curdling scream which startles both of us.

I hate listening to him, but I can't listen to her cry out like that anymore. Phil might be right. Michelle probably thinks the worst is happening to Jen right now... which I don't know how much worse it can really get. I get up from the couch and look at the basement door with disgrace. I don't want to leave Jen down there but what else more can I do right now? I should at least go find Michelle and maybe try to explain everything before this situation gets worse.

"Tell her I'll be back soon." I look at Phil with a glare. "Just don't hurt her anymore. Just stay here and wait for me, I guess," I sigh before I reluctantly leave the house to go look for Michelle.

CHAPTER 15

Michelle

"HELP! OFFICER! SIR! PLEASE I NEED YOUR HELP!" I call out the minute I rush through the front entrance of the police station and toward the front desk.

"Calm down, ma'am. Can I help you?" A male officer in uniform asks from behind the front desk when I stop to take a breath in front of it. From where I parked my car in the parking lot to the entrance of the station isn't that far away from each other but running the few feet in these heels enough of a workout for my tiny feet.

As soon as I heard Jen on the phone, I ran out of work without even telling my boss and sped directly here. I don't know what's going on or where exactly in Townshed she is, but I know I heard her call out for help and to call 911. She wouldn't have done that if she didn't mean it. I could hear it in her voice. *Something is wrong.*

"My best friend is in trouble. I just got off the phone with her," I exhale.

"Okay, calm down, dear. What is your name and what is your friend's name?"

"My name is Michelle. Her name is Jennifer, Jennifer Russo. She's in trouble. She's somewhere in North Townshed at this guy's house. His name is Max. I called her only fifteen minutes ago and I heard her yell call 911, so I raced over here!"

"Come with me," the officer says as he stands up from behind the front desk and leads me into a cubical where a female officer is sitting behind a desk in it.

"Hello, ma'am. I am officer Wheeler. Take a deep breath. Explain to me what's going on from the beginning," she says as she hands me a small white Styrofoam cup of water.

"I don't want this." I shake my head and give it back to her. "My best friend, Jennifer Russo, is in trouble. She is at this guy's house in North Townshed," I repeat what I said to the other cop at the front desk. "She's been dating him for just like, two weeks and he took her there yesterday. When I called to check on her today, she sounded weird, then I asked her if she was okay and that's when I heard her yell out for help."

"What did she exactly yell when she called out for help?" Officer Wheeler asks.

"She yelled the words help and call 911," I say bluntly as I sit up straight and cross my arms at my torso.

"Do you know where she is right now, ma'am?"

"Besides the fact that she is in Townshed somewhere, no." I tilt my head. "That's why I'm here. So, you guys can help me find her."

Officer Wheeler is looking at me with an emotionless expression. The fact that she has no urgency in her body movements is incredibly irritating me.

"Please! You have to look for her," I beg. "She just got out of a coma, not even a couple weeks ago. I'm worried that she's really in danger! She wouldn't have yelled help for no reason."

"Why was she in a coma?" Officer Wheeler asks and her question confuses me.

"Because she was the victim of a hit and run. Why does

that matter?" I blink my eyes as I am trying to contain my composure. *This woman is wasting both mine and Jen's time with all these useless questions.*

"What's her last name again?"

"Russo. Her name is Jennifer Russo," I say as I keep my arms crossed.

"What is Max's last name?" she asks.

"Max, uh," I pause. *Shit.* I don't know his last name. I'm about to pull out my phone and check his social media profile when I remember he doesn't have one. "Uh. I don't know his last name right now, but I know where he works," I sigh.

"Do you think he has her in danger?"

"Well, seeing as she yelled help while she is with him, yes. I do think he does have her in danger," I shoot a glare at her.

"Did she tell you that she needed help from him specifically?" she asks. "Have you tried calling her back?"

I squint my eyes as I stare at her. These questions are appalling to me. "Of course, I called her back, but someone kept sending my call to voicemail. That's why I'm here right now. I figured this is probably a job for you guys; the police," I say.

"Why don't you try calling her again, while you're here?" The officer looks down at my phone in my hand.

"You really want me to call her and possibly put her in more danger?" I huff in disbelief.

Officer Wheeler nods her head, yes. It looks like she thinks that I am joking right now. I'm straight up stunned at how she's handling this. Jen told me how incompetent the cops have been, but I didn't think they wouldn't help me look for her.

"Fine, I'll call her," I sigh as I find Jen's name into my

contacts and put my phone on speaker after I hit call. It doesn't ring and goes straight to voicemail as I expected it would.

"I'm sorry, ma'am," the officer says as she presses her lips in a half smile once she hears Jen's voicemail. "You can't report a missing person until they've been gone for at least twenty-four hours."

"No, no, no. Hold on! I'm not reporting a missing person. I am reporting a person that is in danger - *not missing*." I look at her in shock.

"I'm sorry there's just nothing we can do yet. Unless you have an address or more evidence of where she is, then we can't send anyone to look for her yet."

"Wow," I mumble as I stand up from my chair. "Fine. I'll come back in twenty-four hours so then you guys can begin the search for her dead body," I scowl before I march out of the station.

I never thought that Jen was exaggerating about the police not helping her but now I really understand why she has been so frustrated. *Forest Hill cops are useless assholes.* I need to find her myself. I can't wait a whole twenty-four hours for someone to start looking for her… if they even will. I need to find out more information about Max – starting with his last name.

My cell phone suddenly beeps, and I rush to grab it, hoping that it's a text from Jen but It's not. Instead, it's a notification from my Instagram; ten new likes on the post I put up this morning. It's a picture of me and Jen in the doctor's office from when she got her cast off the other day. As I look at our photo, I think back to how she told me that Max doesn't have social media… but I wonder if his brother does. Jen didn't tell me his brother's name is, but she did say that he lives with Max. If I can find out who he is, along with their last name, then I'm sure I'll be able to find his brother's profile. That is, if he even has social media. Since the only other thing I know about Max is where he works, I decide to drive straight to Stoney's. I'll just have to start there.

Jen

When Phil dropped the plastic cooler on the floor in front of me, my eyes darted open, and my body nearly jolted out of its skin. I must've ridden my energy from all the crying and screaming that I fell asleep at one point. It was either that or I passed out again. I'm not really sure because my head is still throbbing, and it feels like it's getting worse by the minute.

Phil is kneeling in front of me. He slides it closer to me and it lands right against my thigh. I look inside to see a sandwich in a zip lock bag, a bottle of water, and a bag of chips. "This isn't fucking picnic time," I scoff as I kick it away.

"I don't need your attitude. I have enough shit going on right now," he rolls his eyes and pushes it back toward me.

I'm shocked at his tone. He sounds just as frustrated as the cop's always sounded when I was dealing with them. I'm sick of everyone acting like I'm the one that's annoying them; especially Phil. *He's the last person who should be speaking to me this way.*

"*You* have enough on your plate?" My eyes feel like they are popping out of their sockets as I question him. "You're fucking sick, you know that? WHERE IS MAX?" I demand but Phil is beginning to walk away from me now. "WHERE IS HE?" I yell again but he doesn't respond so I burst out into a high-pitched scream.

If he's not going to answer me, then I'm going to annoy the hell out of him until he does. My screams are so loud that my eyes tear up and I can feel my face turn red. Dizziness creeps upon me quickly, but I don't care. I'm screaming until I get my answers from this man. I'm so focused on being as loud as I can that I have my eyes closed.

It isn't until I feel the palm of Phil's hand push up against my lips when I stop yelling. "STOP BEING SO LOUD. NOBODY CAN HEAR YOU BUT ME," he huffs, then pushes my head back while letting go of my mouth. Then he turns to walk back up the steps.

"WAIT!" I call out again.

"What now?" he nearly growls as he turns back around to face me.

"If you're not going to tell me where Max is, then tell me why you drove away that night. Why did you leave me there almost dead? Why didn't you stay and call for help?"

Phil doesn't answer me and starts to walk toward the steps which makes me furious, so I start screaming again.

"STOP YELLING!" Phil masks my screams in a louder tone, and I see him suddenly charging toward me. I can tell that my loudness is angering him even more. *Good. That's what I want. I will be a problem if I have to be. I'm not going down without a fight.*

I stop yelling and stare him directly in his eyes as he stops only a foot away from me. "If you're not going to tell me where Max is or tell me why you left me for dead before, then at least be a human enough to let me go to the damn bathroom," I say sternly as I keep my eyes locked on his.

He looks away after I'm done speaking but doesn't turn to walk up the steps. I can tell he's contemplating it. "I'll only let you go because Max would want me to. Don't try something stupid," he mutters. He unties me, stands me up and pulls my arms behind my back immediately.

I didn't even have time to struggle, he moved so quickly. I can smell alcohol on his breath since he's so close to me which isn't helping my nausea. Holding my hands together, he leads me over to the bathroom, then opens the door and pushes me in by my back.

"I'll be out here," he says, then closes the door while staying on the other side of it.

As if I was expecting you to be somewhere else.

There isn't a window in this bathroom so there's no way I can escape but there has to be something in here that I can use for at least some type of self-defense. I take a moment to think. If I attempt to either throw the toilet tank lid at him or try to hit him with it, I'd have to do it right when he opens the door and hope that he doesn't duck out of the way. I know that he's drunk but he's still very capable of doing things right now and still very strong. I have a big feeling that if I even attempt to try it, I'm going to miss... or he might even be quick enough to use the lid on me.

And I can't let that happen. His strength is no match for mine. Plus, he'll most likely hear me if I go to move the lid because it's heavy. Even if I turn on the faucet, there's barely any pressure that comes out, so the sound of the water running would be loud enough to mask that kind of noise. I can't turn on the shower to mask the noise either because then he'll know somethings up.

I turn on the faucet to disguise the noise when I open the mirror cabinet quietly. There is only a first aid kit filled with bandages and some Q-tips inside.

"Are you done yet?" Phil's voice startles me when he calls out from the other side of the door.

"Uh no. Not yet," I call out as I begin to now rummage through the basket under the sink. In between the old shampoo bottles is a rusted three bladed razor so I take it and wrap a piece of toilet paper around the blade since there is no cover for it, then I stick it carefully down into the cleavage of my bra with the handle facing up. This way, I will be able to pull it out easily whenever I need to. I don't think this razor will help me that much but at least it's *something* right now.

"Hurry up!" Phil shouts, which makes me more nervous.

I look through the basket once more and I almost squeal aloud in excitement when I spot a pair of metal hair cutting scissors. Even though I'd prefer a regular pair of scissors, these are a lot better than a rusted razor. At least these are a bit sharp. I can stab Phil right in the stomach when he opens the door. I'll just have to take him off guard. But, what if I'm too slow and then he ends up using them on me instead? Just like he could if I use the toilet tank lid...*Then, I'll be really fucked.*

"HURRY!" He's getting louder so I have to make a quick decision.

As much as I want to violently assault that pathetic piece of a human being, I am going to hide these in my bra so I can use them to try to cut the rope. If I go with attacking him right now, I think I'm running a greater risk at getting myself hurt and I'm not going to let that happen. Phil is almost a whole foot taller than me and about a hundred more pounds. I need to be smarter than him. I can cut the rope when he's gone and be ready for him at the door next time.

"HURRY!" He's shouting, so I quickly stick the scissors in my bra up against my right boob with the sharp side facing down.

"I'm opening this door if you don't open it right now! You're lucky that I let you even go in on your own!" Phil warns, so I take a deep breath before going to open the bathroom door.

Right as I unlock it, Phil swings the door open, just an inch away from hitting me in the face. He grabs both of my wrists and pulls them in front of me quickly, then he begins to make a tight knot with the rope around them just like before. This time, the knot is *a lot* tighter.

"Sit down, so I can tie you up to the pipe again," he tells me when he brings me in front of it.

I hesitate and try to keep my feet firm on the ground, but he pulls me close to him, tightening his grip firmly around my wrists.

"SIT DOWN NOW," he repeats louder into my face, blasting the smell of alcohol in it. I try to hesitate once more before I reluctantly let him push me down. He grabs the ends of the ropes and begins to tie them back around the same pipe just like before. His body is sideways to me as he is about to finish the knot when I decide to try to pull away from him.

"What is the matter with you? You're making this harder on all of us!" he shouts as he finishes tying the knot around the pipe, then rushes back up the steps and closes the door behind him.

Is he serious? This man has got to be more than just drunk right now. How dare he tell me that I'm the one making this harder! I refuse to go down without a fight. I refuse to let this pathetic excuse of a man win.

With a deep breath and pure hope, I pull the scissors out of my bra and begin to cut at the rope before Phil comes back.

CHAPTER 16

Michelle

When I walk into Stoney's, I'm thankful for the first time ever to see Luke behind the counter near the milkshake machine. "Luke!" I rush over to him breathlessly. "I need your help! Do you know what Max's last name is?" I exhale as I lean forward onto the counter. Jen's always telling me that one day I will regret wearing heels and she's right. I wish she were here right now so she could say that she told me so.

Luke turns around from the milkshake machine while raising his eyebrow. "Who?"

"The new waiter," I impatiently answer.

"Oh yeah, that guy," he says as he shakes his head. "No, I've only worked with him once. Why?"

"So, I'm guessing that means you don't know who his brother is either," I mumble as I direct my eyes behind the counter.

A waitress walks out from the kitchen with a tray of food, passing Luke, so I stop her. "Excuse me, do you know the new waiter, Max?"

She stops walking and raises her eyebrow in the same way Luke did when I asked him. "Who?"

"Ugh, never mind," I mutter as I look away from her and past the counter for anyone in a collared shirt that isn't wearing an apron. "Can I speak to your manager? Is he even here right now?" I ask Luke.

"No. He's not here right now. Why do you want Max's last name so badly?" he looks me up and down with a furrowed eyebrow.

"Because I need it," I say through gritted teeth. "I also need to know where he lives."

"And why do you need all this information about him?" He raises his chin slightly and puts his hands on his hips.

"Because I need it," I say pensively. "It's important... like, life or death. When is your manager coming back?"

"Not until tomorrow morning."

"Okay, so where is his office?" I ask as I impatiently look past his shoulder toward the kitchen behind him.

"I can't tell you that," he laughs.

"Luke. I need this information right now!" I exhale.

His furrowed brow starts to drop but he still has an annoyingly quizzical look on his face.

"Luke, listen to me. I have no time for your games right now," I give him a hard stare. "This is going to sound crazy, but I think Jen is in a lot of danger. She went with Max to his parents' house in Townshed and when I called her today, she yelled out for help before someone hung the phone up, which I think was Max. I don't know where the house is, so I need to find it myself and..." I stop talking when I realize that I am rambling and wasting time because Luke is just staring at me with the same condescending look on his face. His mouth is starting to form into an amusing smirk and it's taking everything in me not to slap it off him.

"Yeah, okay Michelle," he scoffs and goes to turn back towards the kitchen.

Really? Why doesn't anyone believe anything in this damn city?

I abruptly leap over the counter, nearly spraining my ankles when I land in my heels. "Wait!" I follow him into the kitchen, and he turns around, stunned.

"Did you just jump over the counter?" he widens his eyes and exchanges his glance from my four-inch skinny heels to the countertop.

"Yes! Do you think I would do that in these shoes if I was joking?!"

"She can't be back here," another waitress interrupts when she walks past us with a tray of plates in her hand.

"I can be wherever I want to be. Now if you'll excuse us, we were busy." I shoot a glare at her before turning my attention back to Luke. "Luke! I'm serious. Please."

Luke looks at the other waitress. "It's fine, Deborah. I got it." He turns to me. "Come on. Be careful in those shoes back here. No one is supposed to be back here unless they have nonslip shoes. Those are not nonslip," he shakes his head.

"I'll be careful. Let's go," I anxiously motion for him to lead me through the kitchen.

I follow him through to the back of the kitchen and into a small hallway where I see two doors. One is the exit which leads to the outside of the back of the building and the other door parallel to it is the manager's office.

"You're lucky that you know me here, you know. My manager only trusts me with the key since I've been working here the longest," Luke says in a proud voice.

"If he trusts you so much, then why are you still only a waiter and not a manager yet?" I smirk.

"I haven't unlocked this yet, you know." He crosses his arms.

"Okay, okay. I'm sorry. Come on, Jen is waiting." I realize right now is not the time to act snarky but it's just an impulse when it comes to Luke.

Sighing, he walks into the office and sits down in the computer chair behind the desk, then turns around towards the file cabinet behind him. After a few minutes of searching, he pulls out a manilla file and opens it. "So, this is supposed to be Max's file," he says.

"Thank you!" I quickly snatch the paper out of his hand and search for Max's last name and address.

"You're not taking this with you," Luke says, so I pull out my phone to snap a picture of the whole paper. "Woah! No pictures either! You could get me fired! That's a legal document. I'm not even supposed to show you this!" He immediately freaks out but it's too late.

I already took the photo, so I ignore him and put the file back on top of the desk. "Thank you, Luke!" I call out as I run out of the office and through the kitchen. I can hear him muttering but I don't turn around as I walk out of Stoney's and head to my car.

—

I called the phone number in Max's file three times, but it went straight to voicemail every single time, so I drove to the address in his file which is an apartment building in Forest Hill. I am standing in front of his front door on the third floor, and I just knocked but no one answers, so I try to fumble with the doorknob to open it. It doesn't budge so I use my own set of keys to try and break it open, but that doesn't work either.

Just as I am trying to open it with my acrylic nail, the door behind me across the hallway opens and I turn around to see an elderly woman with bright clearly box dyed hair, cherry red hair, peeking her head out from behind it. "Everything okay over there?" she asks.

I am about to tell her to quit being nosey, but then again nosey neighbors normally know things. *She could be useful to me.* "Sorry for the noise," I flash an innocent smile. "I thought this apartment would be unlocked. I'm trying to get in my Airbnb. I'm renting it out for a night. Do you know where the key is?"

The woman smiles as she opens the door a little wider which reveals a bright red robe on her body that matches her hair. "I don't think that's an Airbnb, sweetie. These are only rental apartments. Airbnb is not allowed here."

"Oh, are you sure? I could've sworn this was it. Max and his brother are the hosts. Oh crap, I forgot his brother's name."

"Phil?" she finishes my sentence, just as I hoped she would.

"Oh, I believe so," I pause. "I'm such a ditz. I can't seem to remember their last name..."

"Alverez? Max and Phil Alverez were the hosts? Are you sure?" she questions.

"Ah, yes Alverez! You know what, I'll just give them a call. Sorry to bother you with the noise again," I say with a polite smile before I head back down the hallway to the elevator.

On the way to my car, I begin to search for Phil's profile on my phone. I click on and off the first five accounts until l get to the sixth one and I scroll through the first few posts showing a man who slightly resembles Max. He looks older than Max but only by a few years. Jen did tell me that Phil was his big brother, but she didn't say how much older. This guy looks like he's in his mid-twenties and he's definitely tall like Max is. I can tell by the photo of him standing next to a stop sign.

I'm scrolling by a few more posts when Max's face

catches my eye. It's a photo of him and Phil. They are standing in an empty room with beers in their hands.

The caption reads - **Throwback Thursday with my bro in our first apartment.**

There are no comments, just a couple likes on it and Max isn't tagged. I continue to scroll by more posts when I stop on a picture of Phil, Max, and another woman. Max is standing in the middle of them, and his arm is around her.

The caption reads – **R.I.P Monica. Thank you for making my brother so happy while you were here.**

It was posted only six months ago. I click on Monica's social media handle which is tagged in the caption. Her profile is filled with not only beautiful selfies, but of some photos of her and max too. The last post on her account was put up a year ago which is a selfie in a blue two-piece bikini by the pool. She was almost as skinny as me. Her skin was tan, and her black hair was tied up in a tight top bun.

The first few comments under the picture read -

I miss you so much.

Rest easy. I can't believe you're gone.

I wish I knew how you felt.

Rest in peace, Monica. I wish I knew you weren't happy.

How she felt? Weren't happy? It sounds like Max's girlfriend committed suicide... Okay, I'm pretty sure Jen doesn't know about any of this because she definitely would have told me.

I scroll past five more posts until I see a photo of Monica and Max. The caption under it reads - **Four months today, I love you.** The date it was posted was only a month before her very last post. *That means she died only a month after their anniversary.* There are three comments under it. Two are just heart and kissing emojis while the other is a comment that reads - *cute couple.* There is nothing on Monica's account about being sad. No red flags. All I see is a happy face.

I click back onto Phil's profile and scroll back through his posts. I stop seven posts in on a selfie of him behind a bar when I notice that there is a sign on the door in the back that says Lucky's. I'm not aware of any bars in Forest hill since they aren't my thing and never will be, so I google the name. The only bar that is listed under the names *Lucky's* is on the South end of Townshed.

"No! Are you kidding me?" Just when I click on the address to GPS my way there, my phone shuts off. I didn't charge it last night. I planned to leave it charging while I was at work all day, but I left in such a hurry after I called Jen, that I left my charger at work. I hate that I need to waste more time. However, I have no choice but to go back home, quickly grab my extra cord, and then I can head straight to the bar.

CHAPTER 17
Jen

I think maybe twenty minutes have passed by while I was cutting the rope, but I just stopped because the scissors broke in half. But unfortunately, the rope doesn't even look like it was cut by anything at all. *I'm wasting time and I'm losing more energy.* I was hoping that I'd be able to break myself free from the pipe and take Phil by surprise, but I was mistaken. I should have just gone with my other idea of stabbing him right out of the bathroom… but my instincts told me not to. I thought it would be a better idea, so I could have more time to plan my escape, but now, I need to get him to untie me again because I'm definitely not getting this rope cut.

I put both halves of the scissors back in the side of my bra with the handles facing up. The cooler is still on the floor by me, and I haven't eaten or drank anything out of it yet. I pull it over with my feet, then dump it, so the water bottle can roll out because I can't reach in with my tied-up hands. I take a few sips of it before I kick the bottle across the room in front of me with the lid still off.

"PHIL! PHIL! PHIL!" I shout as loud as I can.

After several yells, the door flings open, and he is marching down the steps within seconds. "I need more water. I knocked over the water bottle on accident. Oops," I shrug.

He gives an exaggeratively loud sigh while rolling his eyes, then turns back around to go back up the steps, leaving the door open behind him. I hear him mumbling in the kitchen before he comes back down with a new water bottle in his hand.

He places it by my feet and then he goes to turn away, but I stop him. "Wait! Wait! Can you take me to the bathroom again?"

I see the whole weight in his body drop from his shoulders down to his back when he dramatically sighs again. "You were just in the bathroom," he groans as he turns to face toward me.

"Well, women go more often than men," I snap with a half smirk.

He eyes me up and down with a furrowed brow. "Don't try to do what you did before. Max doesn't want me to hurt you, so don't make me."

"If Max doesn't want you to hurt me, then where the fuck is he, and why am I still tied up down here?" I snap back.

"Do you want to go to the bathroom or not?" He stops walking toward me.

"Well, if you don't take me, then I'm going to go right here on this floor and then you're going to have to clean it up at one point, so the decisions really on you," I shrug and press my lips into a smirk.

Phil shakes his head in a clearly irritated manner before continuing to walk my way. "Don't try no stupid shit," he mumbles as he unties my hands, then quickly lifts me to my feet. He leads me to the bathroom, holding both of my arms and hands together behind my back. "Be quick," he demands before he pushes me into the bathroom and closes the door, leaving me alone inside.

I go to the sink and look at my reflection through the mirror as I run the water from the faucet. My face is puffy. My eyes are bloodshot, and my hair is such a greasy, sweaty mess that my bangs are practically sticking to my forehead.

Phil is demanding for me to hurry from the other side of the door already, so before I turn off the faucet, I take one half of the scissors out from my bra, leaving the other half still tucked away, then I turn off the water.

Stepping next to the doorway, I press my right shoulder up against the wall so I can see him when he walks through the door. I have the half pair of scissors gripped tightly in between my right palm and thumb. *Now's my only chance.*

"You can open it!" I call out and the door opens a split-second right after. As soon as it does, I step right in front of him. Aiming for his stomach, I stab Phil just above his right hip. I was trying to aim for the side of him, but I think I hit his ribs because the scissors kind of bounced off him a bit, which made me drop them on the floor just now. I felt the scissors go in his skin though. I know I stabbed him, but I didn't do as much damage as I wanted to because he's still standing but he is starting to stumble back away from me out of the bathroom.

Taking advantage of how I took him off guard, I run forward and start to kick him with my right leg in his wounded side. At the same time, I am gripping onto his shirt by his chest to hold on to him, so I don't fall. I kick a few times before I push at him with as much force as I can muster up, then I dart towards the steps. Just as I'm reaching the base of the stairs, Phil tugs me back by my hair and suddenly my eyeline is to the ceiling. Strands of my hair tear off my head while he pulls me down to the floor. I'm squirming to get out of his reach while he's shouting at me to stop but I won't stop moving. Blood from the wound that I inflicted on him is falling down the bottom half of the right side of his body and onto my hair now.

I am kicking and screaming even though I know screaming isn't going to help. At least the kicking does. The more I struggle, the more he's going to have to struggle as well.

"Stop being such a problem," he mutters as I feel his hands grab me from underneath both my armpits.

I'm in the air now, kicking aimlessly like a child as he keeps his hands on me. I'm twisting my body all over, but all it's doing is making Phil angrier. "Bitch, stop moving!" he's grunting but I won't stop struggling.

For a split second only, his hands leave my body when he throws me toward the laundry machines. I put my hands out to break my fall, but the momentum of Phil's throw makes me roll off my palms and on to my right side, landing against the washer.

Every part of my body inside and out is in agonizing pain, especially my spine since it just slammed against the washer. Phil is pacing back and forth by the steps. He's hunched over, holding his wound. I know that I stabbed him, but I didn't do a good enough job at it because he's still standing up. The room is revolving around me, and my armpits still feel like he's gripping underneath them, but I get up anyway.

As soon as I stand, it's like my knees go numb. I try to take a step forward, but I lose balance from the dizziness. I see Phil starting to turn toward me, but my head is spinning so badly that I cannot keep steady on my feet.

"What is wrong with you?" I hear him mumble right

before I catch a glimpse of his fist coming toward my right cheek.

I surprisingly don't get knocked out of consciousness when he punches me... but his punch is still so forceful that it knocks me down to the floor. My ears are starting to ring, and my face is stinging from his punch. I know that tears are rolling down my cheeks, but I can barely feel them through the pain. Phil is reaching for my wrists, but I am too weak to struggle now. As much as I want to get up off this floor and fight him, I physically can't. Before I know it, I'm tied back up to the pipe, alone in the basement and needing a new plan once again.

Phil

I just bandaged up my side but it's still bleeding a lot. She didn't get me in my stomach but she sure as hell stuck my ribs. I'm surprised at the amount of blood that's coming from it. I need Max to get back here right now. I should have just made him help me get the truck out of here before I sent him to look for that Michelle, bitch. I know the police are going to find it now, and if they don't, then someone else will. If someone caught me driving on camera and sent it to Jen, then there must be more that she knows and didn't tell Max.

I wish that I didn't wait for him to get here because of course, he couldn't keep his mouth shut when he saw her. I could have just told him that she left his ass while he was at the store and handled her before he even got here.

Fuck. I regret not doing that.

Excruciating pain shoots through my muscles as I extend my body back against the cushion to reach inside my front pocket for my phone.

"Where the hell are you?" I ask as soon as Max answers.

"I just left our place. There's no cops around," he pauses. "You good? You sound like you're in pain."

"I'd be a hell of a lot better if I didn't just get stabbed," I scoff.

"Wh-- what?" he stutters. "Is Jen alright? Is she hurt?"

"She's fine but she's freaking out, man! I'm not trying to fucking hurt her! Did you find Michelle yet?"

"No, I'm heading back home now. I'm about to get on the highway."

"I don't care about her anymore anyway! You're wasting my time now. Just get back here!" I hang up on him and limp my way into the kitchen for the rest of the Whiskey that I left on the counter. I can hear Jen crying below me, but she isn't as loud as she was before. *Good. She's probably losing energy after the hell she put me through.*

All I wanted to do was keep her here. It was perfect timing when I saw her down in the basement when I was getting the key to the house out of the garage. A little push down the stairs, tie her up, then get both the truck and me the hell out of here. *But no. Max just had to confess everything for me.* I should have just fucked him up, like I just did to Jen. Shit, I'll just finish off this Whiskey while I wait for him to come back, then I'll make him help me get rid of his truck and after that, I'll take care of Jen myself, whether Max likes it or not.

Jen

I can't believe I'm still down here. I was so close to the staircase. I saw the light from the kitchen through the doorway and I'm *so mad* at myself that I didn't succeed

170

in escaping. I wish I stabbed Phil several more times and with more force, but it was a lot harder to do than I planned. My body is throbbing, and my head is massively pounding. The dizziness is still there but it's at least subsided.

If I have another chance out of here, I need to make it count. Phil's injured already, so I need to aim for that spot again. The other half of the broken scissors are still in my bra and the razor is surprisingly in my cleavage too, but the paper I put around it fell off at one point. The blade keeps brushing up against my skin. It's not too sharp to make me bleed but I most definitely can still feel it scratching me. I'll have to use it on him as my last resort... when I'm *really* close to him. One half of the scissors already helped me, so I know the other will too.

"Phil! Phil!" I shout his name multiple times before I finally see the door open.

"What do you want now?" he murmurs as he fumbles slowly down the stairs.

"Bathroom," I mutter.

"Ha! Yeah right," he scoffs as he goes to turn around.

"Wait!" I shout but he is already trying to get up the steps. He is just only halfway up the staircase when I break out into a high-pitched scream. *I'm screaming so loud; my ears become warm.*

My eyes are closed until I feel the palm of his hand swipe me in my right cheek. Since I'm tied to the pipe, his punch stops my body from falling directly to the ground, so I'm kind of just left dangling sadly to the side. The room is revolving again and I'm gasping for breath. The pain is absolutely unbearable. "Please... please," I'm begging him, "bathroom. Please."

While murmuring under his breath, he surprisingly

helps me stand up and unties me from the pipe. I close my eyes the minute I am on my feet to control the spinning in my head before he begins to hobble me toward the bathroom. This time instead of letting me go freely, he takes my hands and brings them to the front of me, then ties them together with the rope.

"How do you expect me to use the bathroom when my hands are tied?" I sigh.

"Figure it out," he mumbles before shoving me through the doorway.

After he pushes me inside of the bathroom, I have to catch myself against the sink to keep steady. I actually do have to use the bathroom this time, so I quickly go before I go back to the sink and turn on the water. The second I turn it on, Phil yells at me to hurry but I don't answer him. I open the cabinet under the sink quickly and look through the basket again. The toilet paper rolls will do me no good, and there are only a few shampoo bottles which are basically all empty except for one. There's a little less than half the shampoo left in it, so I take it and tip it over to shake it a few times until the soap falls toward the lid.

"HURRY!" He's rushing me from the other side of the door and it's not helping.

With a deep breath, I turn off the water and Phil immediately yells, "are you done now? I'm busting this door open in the next five seconds if you don't get the hell out of there!"

Standing in front of the door, I take a second to exhale. My heart is racing, and my head is throbbing. I am holding the bottle, along with the other half pair of scissors that I pulled out of my bra, in both of my hands and I'm praying that I don't drop them. My hands are sweaty and they're trembling but I'm still keeping this bottle steady no matter what. After another deep exhale, I finally call out, "Okay, you can open the door now!"

The door flings open almost immediately and at the same time, Phil is already rushing in the doorway giving me no time to take a step toward him. Aiming the bottle towards his face, I squeeze it and the shampoo shoots out just enough to take him off guard again.

"You bitch," he grunts as he starts to back out of the bathroom trying to wipe the soap off his face.

While he does, I go straight towards his wounded right side with the scissors and I stab him with as much force as I can. He is crouching over and backing away into the bathroom more. He has one hand on his wounded side, while the other is still fumbling to wipe the soap out of his face. He can't even stand up straight.

Without hesitation, I charge towards him, my arms stretched out with my tied-up hands facing his chest. I grab onto his shirt, and I begin to kick him with my right leg. I am doing my best to aim my barefoot directly at his wound even though it is covered by a bandage. My kicks are so powerful that the bandage is beginning to fall off.

Along with his flesh in between my toes, blood is running all down my leg now. I can feel it, but I don't stop kicking. I have never kicked anyone before, but it doesn't feel new to me. It feels good, especially since it's Phil who I'm kicking. *Finally, I'm the one causing him pain.*

I abruptly feel his hand catch me by my right ankle when I kick at him again, making me almost fall down but I don't let it happen. I'm still gripping onto his shirt so tightly that it's being stretched around his neck and it's taking all the strength in me to keep balance on my left leg. My mouth is dry from barely drinking a thing all day, but I still manage to come up with enough saliva in my mouth to spit at him. When I do, it hits his nose, startling him which makes him finally drop my leg. I stumble back to catch my balance and at the same time, he's rushing toward me with his head low and one hand over his wounded side. He's going right for my waist.

Just as I feel his hands grip my hips, I reach down and bite the left tip of his ear. He screams and staggers back away from me. I lunge at him with my tied-up palms toward his chest and surprisingly, I make him fall to the ground with one good push. I go for the razor in my bra but it's not there anymore so instead I head toward the steps.

There's no way I'm letting this psycho get a hold of me again.

I see a shovel hanging on the wall at the end of the stairway as I try to dizzily stagger over to it. Just as I grab it off the wall, the bottom of my shirt near my lower back gets tugged and I fall down on my stomach. I grabbed the shovel in time, but it fell out of my hands and onto the floor next to me with the digging side right next to my head.

Phil's heavy body is on my lower back pulling at my shirt and hips, but it doesn't stop me from grabbing the shovel again. Although, I wish that the digging side fell next to him instead of my head, I still push the shovel back until I feel the handle side hit him and his hands slide off me seconds later. Just as I feel my shirt loosen, I roll onto my back to see that Phil's lying on his stomach almost in a cradle like position. I think I hit him right in the left shoulder because he's grabbing onto it and grunting.

Although I'm in unbelievable agonizing pain, I don't plan on giving him any time to try to even get back up. I stand up to my feet, amid the dizziness and immediately slam the digging side of the shovel right on where I stabbed him earlier.

But I don't stop there. I lift it away from him, and then I slam it down on top of his left shoulder. I lift it one last time with the little strength that I have left, and then I drop it down on the left side of his head. Finally, he stops moving.

CHAPTER 18

Jen

I have no more strength to hit Phil anymore, but... I don't think I need to worry about that because he hasn't moved after I just slammed his head with the shovel. Phil left the basement door open just slightly enough before he came down here. I can see a sliver of light coming from the kitchen through the doorway. Between the dizziness and dehydration in me, I barely have the strength to keep myself standing but I know I need to make it up those steps and get the hell out of here.

Just as I'm ready to steady myself and go toward the stairs, more light starts to flood in as the door opens wider and Max starts to walk through the doorway. "What... what did you do?" he gasps when he gets down the middle of the steps and see's Phil lying by the bottom of the stairs.

"Just let me go home," I beg through sobs as I back away from Phil and over to the window while Max starts rushing down the steps. "Max, please... just let me go home!"

"Fuck, fuck..." I hear him cursing under his breath, as he rushes over to Phil.

"I had to... I had to hurt him," I go to say but Max is already picking up Phil and putting him over his shoulder. He rushes up the stairs with him, leaving a trail of Phil's blood on the steps behind him.

"Wait," I beg as I try to run after him but I'm too dizzy to move as fast as he is.

I'm not even halfway up the steps when he's already rushing through the doorway and closing the door behind him. I stumble up only seconds after it closes, but when I go to open it... it's locked. I am pulling at the doorknob but it's not budging and after only three attempts of tugging at it, I have to stop because I'm getting dizzier. Seconds after I sit down, I hear the front door slam.

While grabbing onto the railing of the staircase, I stand back up and begin to slowly walk down the steps. I make my way over to the window and climb on top of the ladder that I left in front of it from earlier. Right when I peer out of it, I see Max's SUV backing out of the driveway. He just left me locked down here in the basement alone again.

Max

This wasn't supposed to happen... None of this was supposed to happen.

I just laid Phil down in the backseat of my SUV. He's breathing but he's not moving. I am taking him to the emergency room. He needs medical attention as soon as possible. *I'm not going to let him die like I let Monica.*

His body is so limp in my backseat, and it reminds me of what Monica looked like when I found her except her skin was a lot paler. I never wanted to re-live that memory again but now I'm doing it all over with my brother only a year later. I'm in shock that Jen went this far... but I also don't blame her. She was fucking tied up to a water heater.

I know she was probably scared to death. It looked like she went through hell when I just saw her.

Phil really lost his damn mind this time… but then again, maybe I have too. I kind of let things get this far to begin with. *All this is my fault.* I shouldn't have ever called Phil in the first place or even left the house to begin with. I was listening to him once again when I knew that I shouldn't be. I should have stayed at the house with Jen… I should have protected her.

"Wake up! Bro, wake up!" I'm reaching back to shake him with my right arm while my left is controlling the steering wheel. "Bro! Wake up! Please!" I'm begging him to stay awake the whole way there.

We are just about half a mile away from the hospital when I hear him groan and I look in the rearview mirror to see him trying to open his eyes. "What… what the-?" he grunts in agony when he realizes that he's in my backseat.

"Don't move, man. Here, put this on your stomach and hold your hand over it. You need to stop the blood." I give him a towel that I brought with me from the bathroom in the house. He takes it but he can't hold it steady enough to keep on his stomach. It falls off him and onto the floor of my SUV. His head keeps falling back and it's a struggle for him to breathe.

"Man, you got to stay awake with me," I say but I can tell that it's difficult for him. He keeps shutting his eyes. I think he's falling in and out of consciousness. "I don't know what the fuck went on down there between you two, but I'm taking you to the hospital."

"No," he murmurs. "Pull over." He just opened his eyes wider than he has so far and it looks like it hurt him because he's really wincing from the pain now.

"What do you mean, no? You're losing a lot of blood.

You're going to pass out again," I argue with him as I pull the SUV into the entrance of the hospital parking lot. "I'm already here."

"Pull over," he repeats but I ignore him and continue driving up toward the emergency room.

"My phone," he stammers in between gasps of breath.

"What? What are you talking about?" I look at him through my middle rear-view mirror.

I see Phil trying to sit up, but he fails. "Our texts. You need to know."

Instead of pulling straight up to the emergency entrance, I make a left away from it and into the visitor parking lot off to the side of the building. After I quickly park my SUV in the first empty spot that I find, I turn around to face him. "What are you talking about, man?"

Wincing, Phil struggles to reach in his left pocket for his cell phone and I take it from him, then I use his index finger on the fingerprint scanner on the back of the phone to unlock it.

"What about your texts?" I ask, confused.

"Monica," he murmurs, "I'm sorry."

I go directly into his text messages and look for Monica's name. I never looked at her phone because I never thought I needed to, that's how much I trusted her. I begin to read through the message history between them and my heart feels like it drops down to my feet. The date on their last text conversation is on the same day she died.

M - Phil, I can't do this anymore. Do you still have those pills you offered me? I just can't keep living this way. I think it's time.

P - Can I join you?

M - You can't do that to Max. He needs you. Please, just bring me them as soon as you can.

P – I'll be on my way soon.

I feel sick to my stomach. I wonder if this is how Jen felt when she first saw me walk down into the basement after Phil tied her to the pipe - betrayed, stunned, angered, sad... probably mostly confused. I scroll up through the thread of earlier messages between them. Just two weeks prior to their last message, she texted him a few times that she was crying in the middle of the night. He texted her back that she's beautiful and that everything will be okay. He can talk to her whenever she didn't want to talk to me. I keep scrolling and I just can't take it anymore when I see a line of text from him that reads - *If you were with me, then maybe you'd feel happier instead.*

Phil and Monica seemed so close, almost too close at times, but I always dismissed it. I just thought that they had a great friendship which is what I wanted, for my brother and girlfriend to get along, but not in this way. I knew that Monica felt sad, but she never told me it was so bad. I never knew until after she died.

But Phil knew. He knew the whole time and he never told me. He didn't even try to help her with her depression. He did the complete opposite. He texted the words; *can I join you?* That means he knew what she was planning on doing. She asked him for the pills, and he ran right over with them. I should have known that they came from him. I feel like an idiot to not realize before. I thought Phil stopped selling a few years ago... but I guess I was wrong.

There wasn't a pill bottle by her or even a note when I showed up. I only found out later from her parents that

EVERYTHING LED ME TO YOU

she died from an overdose on an antidepressant which they found out when they did the coroner report. Along with her parents and the police, they asked me if I knew anything about her taking pills or where she got them, but I truthfully had no idea. I didn't think they came from Phil. I was just as confused and hurt as everyone else. I had been feeling that way up until now... and Phil knew that too. He saw how I grieved this past year. *He saw what I went through.* I was so confused about everything... but now I'm angry. I'm angry at Phil. Monica didn't need to die. Just like Jen didn't need to get tied up.

Fuck! Jen! I can't let her get hurt anymore...

I pull my SUV out of the parking spot and up to the front of the emergency room entrance, then get out of my car to open the backseat door.

One nurse is starting to speak to me as I watch two others pull Phil out of the backseat and onto a stretcher. "Sir, can you tell me what happened?"

"Uh," I stutter as I hesitate for a moment. "I-I found him outside on the road when I was driving. I don't know who he is."

The nurse tells me to wait but I get back in my SUV and drive away instead.

CHAPTER 19
Jen

I was able to cut the rope from around my wrists by cutting it on the digging side of the shovel, but I wasn't able to break the door open when I slammed it against the doorknob. I had to stop after a few times because I am becoming progressively weaker. I tried to pick the lock with some screwdrivers that I just found but I just gave up because nothing worked.

The window wouldn't budge when I first tried to open it earlier, but I didn't really have much time to keep trying before I thought I saw Max. If I couldn't get the door to break open, then I'll have to break the window. I shouldn't stand on top of the ladder because I won't have enough strength to hold the shovel up and be able to keep myself steady at the same time, so I have to try to break the window from the ground. It's only about a foot higher than me.

After I move the ladder out of the way, I begin to swing the shovel at the window. It hurts like hell to lift my arms, but I do it anyways. To my disappointment, the glass doesn't break. Instead, the shovel bounces off the window and it makes me stumble back a foot. I steady my feet before I go to try again. My muscles and limbs ache with every swing, but I keep going. The window is cracking but it's not breaking. I'm losing more strength and I'm getting dizzier. I have to stop for a moment to take a breather, before I stand firmly with both of my feet planted on the floor again.

I lunge the shovel at the window three more times and on the third hit, it finally shatters. The glass falls into the basement and outside of the window. For the first time in hours, I feel myself smile. *I'm crying from happiness. I'm finally breaking out of here!*

So much adrenaline is rushing through me now that I don't even feel the pain in my body. Glass shards are loose on the ground outside and around the perimeter of the windows, but I don't care about getting cut.

Just as I am climbing out the window, I start to hear sirens in the distance. Seconds later, they become louder, and I see a Townshed police car quickly pulling into the driveway. Two more police cars are following behind. An officer comes out of the first car and begins to run toward me. She has her hand on her weapon on her side while the two other officers are beginning to run behind her. Although every part of my arms ache, I close my eyes and hold up my hands as high as I can, to let them know that I am innocent.

—

It's been a few minutes since the police saw me crawling out of the window. A paramedic draped a heavy blanket over my shoulders and is cleaning the blood off my wrists while putting some ointment and bandages over them. I've been sitting on the front porch of the house, and I haven't gone back inside since I broke free from the basement. I am hunched over since it's the only way to keep my back from aching so badly. Now that my body is calm and the adrenaline of escaping is gone, I feel every single inch of my muscles and bones throb.

One of the police officers just walked up to me. She looks like a ten year younger and skinnier version of Officer Rodriguez. The same type of dry facial expression rests on her face.

"I am Officer Marien. Can you tell me your name please, ma'am?" she asks while a paramedic begins to check my head, and another checks my back out.

"Jen Russo," I mutter. I am staring out into the vacant land across the street from Max's house. I don't think I can move my eyesight off anything else right now. I can barely even direct my attention to the officer or the paramedic.

"Can you tell me what happened here?" Officer Marien asks.

"Wh-- where's Michelle?" I break my gaze from the land ahead of me up to the officer who is now giving me a bizarre look.

"Who? No one else is in the house. We did a thorough check through. You were the only one here," she responds.

"No," I shake my head. "I'm talking about my best friend. Didn't she call you guys to come save me?"

"No, I don't think it was her unless she called in as anonymous," Officer Marien answers.

"What?"

"An anonymous person called 911 and notified us that someone was in danger at this address. They didn't leave a name," she tells me.

"Anonymous?" I repeat under my breath more so to myself, than to the officer.

If it wasn't Michelle, then...the only person who I think it could be... is Max.

But why would he call in as anonymous?

"Jen, I can tell that you've been through a lot. You can take your time, but I do need you to tell me what happened here, so I can help you." Officer Marien's voice breaks me from my thoughts.

"Uh," I hesitate. "I, Uh, I-I-I," I keep stuttering as I don't know how to really begin or what to even tell her.

"It's okay. Take a deep breath," she tells me. "Let's start with this house. Do you live here?"

I shake my head, no.

"Whose house is this? How did you get here?"

"Uh, I came here with Max... He told me that it was his parent's house."

"Okay, who is Max? Did Max hurt you?"

"He -- he didn't hurt me," I wince when the paramedic grabs hold of my right forearm to finish bandaging it. I felt the sting from the ointments but that's no match to the rest of the pain that I feel from getting hit in the face and thrown around so many times.

"Can you tell me who tied your hands together, Jen?" Officer Marien continues.

"Max-- Max's brother," I mumble.

"What's his brother's name?"

"Phil," I gulp because when I say his name, I realize that he's probably dead right now and I'm the cause of it.

Shit. How the hell can I explain that to her though? How can I explain any of this?

"Who is Max?" she asks me again. "Do you know where Max and Phil are right now?"

"I... I don't know," I answer as I start gasping for air. *Shit. Now I'm starting to panic again.* Suddenly I'm hyperventilating, and I can't control it. The last moments with Phil are flashing in my head and I can't tell her about them. It's hard to breathe.

I feel like I'm having a panic attack, but I think this actually might be a heart attack because I'm *really* struggling to breathe now. Everything in my body is tight, especially my chest. I can't keep this blanket on me anymore. It's making me sweat so I throw it off my shoulders as fast as I can. I'm still hyperventilating, and everything is spinning. I know I'm sitting but I feel like I'm about to fall over. I can hear the paramedics talking but I don't know what they're saying.

There is something over my mouth now. In my blurry vision, I think it is an oxygen mask. I can hear someone telling me to calm down, but I don't think that is helping me. Before I know it, I am being escorted into the ambulance as I hear a paramedic tell me that they are taking me to North Townshed's hospital.

CHAPTER 20

I just woke up to the voices of a female and a man talking to each other next to me, so I try to open my eyes, but I can barely get my right one to open. A female nurse stands at the foot of the bed in front of me, behind a computer while a male nurse is to the right of my bed side.

"Hi, there. I'm your nurse, Jamie. You are at North Townshed Memorial. Can you tell me your name?" the nurse behind the computer says.

I look at her then I move my head to the right toward the male voice I heard. "Ugh," I recoil in agony when I turn my neck and a sharp pain strikes through it.

"Try to keep your head still," the male nurse says. "My name is Jeremy. I'm just checking your vitals, right now."

I move my hand to my forehead, and I feel a large bandage on it. When I go to sit up, a shooting pain runs through my right shoulder and Jeremy stops me right away.

"I wouldn't do that," he says. "Try to stay still."

"Can you please tell me your name?" Jamie repeats.

"Um… Dan," I grunt.

"What is your last name?"

"Uh," I clear my throat. "Canner… Dan Canner."

"Dan, you've got three right cracked ribs, some internal bruising and bleeding, a laceration on your right side, a

187

broken collar bone, and a torn rotator cuff in your right shoulder. We are getting ready to take you into surgery. I need you to answer some questions for me first, okay? Now, do you have any allergies to any medications that I need to know about?"

I shake my head, no.

"Have you gone through any recent surgeries, injections, falls, accidents, or injuries in the past six months?"

I shake my head, no. "How did I get here?"

"Somebody dropped you off. They said they found you on the side of the road. You've been in and out of consciousness for a little while."

Fuck, where the hell did Max go?

"Do you remember how you got your injuries?"

"I-- I think I got jumped," I lie. "I was jogging. Some guys jumped me."

"You always go jogging in jeans Dan?" Jamie asks as she continues to type on her keyboard.

"Mhmm," I mumble.

"Did you know these guys that jumped you?" she asks.

I shake my head, no.

"Okay. You can make a report with the police after you come back from surgery," she tells me as she begins to lift my bed and roll it out of the room and into the hallway with the other nurse.

"No, no, that's okay," I quickly say. "I don't even know what the guys looked like. I just saw their feet."

"Alright, we will worry about that when you come out of surgery, sweetie," she says as they begin to roll my bed out of the room.

"Do you have an emergency contact that you would like me to call for you, Dan?" Jamie asks as they wheel me down the hall.

"Uh, that's okay. How long do I have to stay here?"

"The doctor will let you know once your scans come back," she answers as we make a right at the end of the hallway. I look all around me for Max, but I don't see him anywhere.

When we are approaching the elevators down the hall, I have to blink a few times once I get wheeled by a patient's room. Just as a doctor is walking into it... I think I catch a glimpse of Jen sitting in bed. If she's here, then that means I'm really screwed now.

Jen

Again, it's almost like I'm reliving the day I awoke out of my coma but this time I'm fully aware of everything around me and I can recall everything that happened to me in the past day. The only thing that I cannot recall too clearly is the ride in the ambulance over to the hospital. I didn't have a heart attack like I originally thought I was having back at the house, but I did have a major panic attack. I was panicking so hard that I didn't even realize we were at the hospital until I was being wheeled through the emergency room on a stretcher.

Amid it all, I guess I managed to tell the paramedics that I had been in a coma a few weeks ago because telling them that brought me right in to get a head scan as soon as I got here. After that, I finished getting all the scans that I needed on the rest of my body, and I immediately made sure that no one called my emergency contact which is my mother. I don't need my parents knowing what went on yet because I still can't even fathom what has happened. I did ask the paramedics, or the nurse (I can't really remember because I was so out of it) if I could call Michelle and they told me that I would be able to soon.

I'm sitting up in a hospital bed now. My back is still hurting and my heads pounding but it's not as bad as it was when I was back at the house. Since I have an IV in my arm for fluids, I don't feel nauseous anymore and they already gave me some medicine to ease the pain. Although, I think whatever they gave me is actually making me more tired rather than easing the pain because I'm still hurting everywhere and I'm really drowsy. Good thing is, that I am no longer panicking but I feel really... I guess you could say, strange. I know I'm physically here but mentally, I'm not so sure.

There's a doctor standing at the foot of the bed in front of me, but I don't know how long he's been standing there. I don't even remember him walking in the room. He's been talking but I have no clue what he's been saying until now.

"So, beside some bruising and the herniated disk in your lower back, all other test results came back fine. I gave you some medicine just to calm your nerves along with some morphine. Use it as needed for the pain," he says as he gestures toward my IV stand. "I'll be back in to monitor you after Officer Marien finishes her report."

Herniated disk? Morphine? Officer Marien is still here?

I don't even have a second to myself to think before Officer Marien walks through the door as the doctor walks out. Instead of Officer Rodriguez who didn't seem to care much about my accident, Officer Marien is looking way more intrigued. She looks even more intrigued than she did back at the house.

"Can I call my best friend?" I ask as I look at the phone

on the table beside me while she approaches the side of my bed.

"Yes, you can in a few minutes, Jen. I just need you to answer a few more questions for me first, that way I can understand what happened to you," she answers as she stands by the right of my bedside with her notepad. "You said the house you were in was Max's parent's house?"

I nod my head, yes.

"Okay. So, tell me who Max is? Do you know his last name?"

"Uh, his last name is Alverez. I was dating him."

"So, he was your boyfriend?"

"Uh, yeah..." I answer but then I shake my head no, quickly. "Actually no, not yet. I don't know. We just started dating."

"Did Max hurt you?"

I hesitate before I sigh, "No... Phil did."

"How did you end up in the basement?" she continues with her questions.

"I was putting the hiking gear away when I got locked in."

"How did you get locked in?"

I shrug my shoulders because I am honestly not sure now. I thought I locked myself in at first but after Phil pushed me down the steps, I thought it was him who initially locked me in. But now... I'm not so sure that it was him because Max left me locked in the last time that I saw him too.

"I just went to open the door to leave when I was done putting the stuff away and it was locked. I don't know." I roll my eyes unintentionally when I answer because I'm just as confused as this cop is.

"Around what time was that?" Officer Marien

continues her questions.

"Maybe 1:00 p.m., I think."

"Why were you at the house in the first place?"

"I was supposed to spend the weekend with Max there," I groan.

"When did you first arrive?"

"Yesterday morning."

"So, you went to the house willingly with Max?"

I nod, yes as I scrunch my forehead. I don't like how she just used the word *willingly*.

"Did you know that Phil was going to be at the house too?" she continues.

I shake my head, no.

"And when was the first time you encountered Phil?"

"When I first saw him through the basement window. I was looking out of it for Max to come back from the store so he can unlock the basement door for me. I thought I saw him pulling the garage door down..." I pause as I think back to the moment.

I really thought that it was Max who was walking toward me. If only I stayed in front of the window longer, I would've noticed that it wasn't him. Then maybe, I could've avoided all this. Maybe, I could have been ready for him.

"Ma'am, I am just trying to get a better understanding of what happened," Officer Marien says before I can go on. Her tone does not sound as frustrated as Officer Rodriguez's had sounded, but it does sound contemplative. I'm not sure if she's on my side or if she thinks something else of me because the tone in her voice isn't very clear.

I clear my throat before I go on. "I went up the stairs to meet him at the door right after that because I thought he was coming to unlock it but when the door opened... that's when I realized it wasn't Max. It was Phil... Then he pushed me down the stairs," I pause to wipe tears away from my eyes as they are beginning to roll down my cheeks. "I think I knocked out when I fell because I woke up tied to the pipe of the water heater. I don't even remember him doing it."

"Did you know Phil prior to that encounter?" Officer Marien continues writing on her notepad.

I shake my head, no.

"So," Officer Marien pauses as she exchanges a look from her notepad to me. "You got locked in the basement while putting hiking gear away around 1:00 p.m., correct?"

I nod my head, yes.

"Was anyone else in the house when you were doing that? You said you were waiting for Max to come back from the store. When did he leave to go there?"

"Max left... maybe, about half an hour before that. I took a shower and cleaned up before I went down to the basement. I was alone in the house," I say, and more tears fall down my face as I think about the moments with Max before everything happened. I was having such a good time and it got ruined so unbelievably quickly. The more I think about everything, the more I keep crying.

"Okay, we're almost done here Jennifer. Just a few more questions," she says. "How did you break free from the pipe?"

Through sobs and stutters, I try to explain, "Phil-- Phil untied me from it," I hesitate before I go on to tell her what I really did to him. She is still looking at me with questionable eyes and I don't like it. I never had a problem or really an opinion about the police before my accident, but now I do. I don't trust them, and my instincts are telling me that I should not give this officer any more detail about what really happened with Phil.

"Um, so then... when I opened the door to walk out of the bathroom, I charged right at him and pushed him down. He wasn't expecting it, so he fell backward on the floor," I pause. "I tried to run past him to go up the steps, but he caught me by grabbing the back of my shirt and then he threw me against the washing machines," I stop talking to exhale as I look at Officer Marien. She is fiercely writing away on her notepad.

A good, few seconds of silence from me passes before she looks up and says, "and then what happened?"

"Uh," I swallow. "After he threw me, he ran up the steps and left the basement... but he didn't tie me up to the pipe again. He just left me alone down there, so I kept trying to break the window. Then when I finally did break it and crawled out... you guys showed up."

"Jen," Officer Marien says as she stops writing, then gives me a deep stare. "There was quite a bit of blood in the house, and it doesn't seem to be yours."

I have nothing to say but just stare at her. I shrug my shoulders, keeping my lips pressed together. I knew I shouldn't have answered any of these questions.

Officer Marien takes a second to look at me before she asks, "Where was Max during all of this? Where is Max and Phil right now?"

I shrug my shoulders again. "Honestly, I don't know."

Officer Marien gives me a perplexing look but doesn't acknowledge what I said. Instead, she asks, "So to clarify, Jen, tell me... when was the last time you saw Max."

"Before he went to the store after our hike," I lie. I'm not going to tell her that the last time I saw him was when he grabbed Phil's dead body and ran up the steps with him. Then she will know I killed him which means she'll know that I lied just now and that will just make her ask me more questions that I don't have solid answers to.

"Do you have Max's phone number to contact him?"

"No. Phil took my phone," I sigh.

"Do you know why Phil did this to you?" she continues.

I think about telling her that Phil crashed into me, but I have no proof. Officer Marien is a Townshed cop. Townshed police don't have my case file, so they aren't familiar with it. I only have Phil and Max's words but they're both not here. I don't even have my cell phone to show her the text from Natalie or the videos that I took of the security cameras. I have nothing to back up my story so rather than answering her, I just keep my head low and shrug my shoulders. I just want all this questioning to stop already. *I want to call Michelle and to go home.*

"Ma'am, I can see that you've been through a lot, but I need to have a better understanding of everything that happened. Have you ever met Phil before this?"

"No," I mumble.

"How did you know that Phil is Max's brother, then?"

"Um, Phil told me," I sigh and suddenly, I'm bursting out into more uncontrollable tears. *I can't handle this anymore.* "Can I call my best friend now? Please? I don't have any more answers. I don't know why Phil did this to me or where both Max and him are. I just want to go home," I'm nearly begging through sobs. I feel another panic attack coming on and I think Officer Marien is noticing because she finally just put her notepad away.

"Deep breaths, Jennifer. We are almost done here. I am going to look for Phil, Max, and the owners of the property as well. Do you know what Max's parent's names are or anything about them, besides the fact that they own the house?"

"Max told me they died. I think the house is his or it's Phil's. I don't know."

"When I find Max and Phil, would you like to press charges on both of them?" she asks.

"Uh," I hesitate as I picture Max's stunned expression when he saw Phil on the floor and his quick actions to save him. It was the same look on his face when he saw me tied up to the pipe. He not only looked stunned, but also confused...

He said he wanted to untie me, but Phil did stop him.

Although, he really didn't try that hard to fight him...

"Ma'am?" Officer Marien is trying to break me from my thoughts by rushing my answer. "If Max hurt you too, then I'd suggest you tell me the truth."

But Max never hurt me. I have no idea where he was the entire time when I was down there... but I think he called the cops to save me, even though he did leave me locked in the basement the last time. *It had to be him who called.* It wasn't Michelle and it couldn't have been Phil. I don't know what I want Officer Marien to do about Max, but I do know that I want her to leave me alone already.

"Max didn't hurt me. I'll press charges on Phil," I gulp. *Whether I say yes or no to pressing charges on Phil, I don't think it will make a difference because I'm ninety-nine percent sure that he's dead... wherever he is right now.*

"Okay, ma'am. I am still going to look for Max just for questioning. Please contact me if you hear from him. Otherwise, I will call you," Officer Marien says before leaving me her card.

I set the card down on the table beside me and I reach over to the hospital phone to call Michelle. "It's me," I say

EVERYTHING LED ME TO YOU

as soon as she answers the phone.

"Are you okay?" she gasps. I can hear the panic in her voice already.

"I'm fine now. I'm in North Townshed's hospital," I say as I wipe tears from my eyes. I am trying not to cry and speak in coherent sentences, so I don't freak her out but it's more and more difficult with every word.

"What happened? I heard you on the phone! I went straight to the police, but they didn't help me at all. They told me that I had to wait twenty-four hours before they could do anything! What happened to you? Where is Max? Why are you in the hospital?" The questions are beginning to pour out of her so quickly that I can barely get a word in.

"I have no idea where he is," I answer, and I begin to start hyperventilating. I don't even know how or where to start. "Just get here please... Max's brother locked me in the basement. The cops just left my room." I have to stop to gasp for air. "Please just get here. I'll explain more in person. I don't have my phone. His brother took it."

A good few seconds of silence pass before Michelle answers in stutters. "Uh, o--okay, I'm leaving my apartment now." I can hear the urgency in her voice before she hangs up.

Thirty minutes later, Michelle came running into my room. She immediately hugged me and nearly screamed when she saw me which did not help my headache, but it did make me slightly laugh. I've already explained everything to her from the moment I went down in the basement and to Max's confession for Phil and how I believe that I killed him. When I am done telling her everything, her tan skin has turned basically almost pale.

"Jen," she says with her eyebrows narrowed. "You

didn't tell the cops any of what you just told me at all?"

"I told them a variation," I say softly.

"Jen..." Her face is full of worry.

"I couldn't tell them the whole truth, Michelle! I still have no proof that it was Phil who crashed into me, and these are Townshed cops," I lower my voice even more. "They don't even have my case file. There would have been no point in telling them the truth. I have zero proof of anything."

"Okay, but-- but..." she stammers before lowering her voice to almost a whisper like mine. "You just said you think you killed him. There must have been blood everywhere. I mean, you just told me you beat him to death with a shovel and stabbed him... How much blood was there? The cops didn't question you about that?"

"Well, yeah... the officer mentioned it but I just kind of shrugged it off and she changed the subject. There wasn't like a shit ton of blood everywhere, but I guess there was some... I don't know," I sigh as I think back to Phil's blood on the basement floor and the drops of it on the staircase.

"Okay, but you still should have told them what you did to Phil. You really think you're going to get away with killing a man?" she's looking at me with an equal amount of worry and confusion.

"I don't know what I was thinking! I just couldn't tell that officer what I did... especially not after the way she was looking at me," I pause. "I'd probably be in handcuffs right now if I told her the truth. I guess my instincts told me to lie, I don't know," I shrug. "I just don't trust the police anymore... not after what I've been through with Forest Hill's cops. They clearly don't do their jobs as well as they're supposed to. Look at what happened when you went to them to get me help. They did nothing. They told you to wait a whole day."

"Okay, you're right." Michelle is beginning to pace beside my bed as she agrees with me. She shakes her head as I can see that everything that I'm telling her is slowly starting to sink in. "I guess you have a point but now this is an open case, right? What do you think is going to happen when they eventually do find Phil and Max?"

I shrug my shoulders as I give her a hopeless look.

"Okay, so let's get back to Max," Michelle says when she sits down on the side of my bed. "So, as soon as he saw you, he just confessed everything? Just like that? I don't get it."

"Sort of... I don't know if he knew I was down there before that because he looked really shocked when he saw me," I pause as I think about the minute, I saw him come through the door and the expression on his face. "He told me that he realized Phil crashed into me after he looked through my texts at lunch. Phil was blocking him by standing at the end of the steps the whole time. He never even let Max come near me."

"Why was he looking through your messages to begin with?" Michelle crosses her arms at her torso.

"Ugh, I don't know!" I snap as I roll my eyes even though I don't mean to give her an attitude.

"Look, I'm sorry that I'm asking you all these questions, but this is all really confusing, Jen."

"I know," I sigh. "It's confusing to me too. Max said he was going to untie me, but Phil stopped him when he tried to go toward me. Then you called and that's when Phil found my phone behind the washer. After he hung up on you, he just pushed Max right up the steps. It all happened so fast. That was the last time I saw him before he came back and then left with Phil."

"So, when Max came back to the basement the second time... after you... you know," she pauses insinuating what I did to Phil, "he should have helped you, but he didn't Jen. You told me that he still left you locked down there. Why didn't you tell the cops that?"

"Because then I would've had to explain that he left with Phil's dead body," I sigh. "I don't know why I even answered any questions to begin with. I'm just really confused. Max and I were having such a perfect weekend before everything," I pause to wipe my eyes. I'm not sure if I'm crying because of the pain in my body or because of just everything that happened altogether. "Max never actually physically harmed me, and I believe that he called the police to save me."

"Okay, but if he closed the basement door and it locked behind him when he took Phil away, then he locked you in on purpose, Jen. I don't care if you think he called for help."

"I don't know," I say as I attempt to sit up in the bed but the pain in my lower back stops me from moving quickly. "Nothing makes sense to me except that he was the anonymous caller. If I didn't believe that, then I would have given the officer a different story, I really would have... but my instincts are telling me otherwise."

Michelle looks at me and tilts her to the left side head a bit. "Jen, do you know about Monica?"

"Who?" I look at her perplexed. "Who is that?"

"His ex-girlfriend," she says as she takes out her phone from her purse. She begins to tell me about her while showing me both hers and Phil's social media accounts. "Max never mentioned her to you at all?" she questions.

I shake my head no, as I hold her phone in my hands and I look at Monica's profile. "Never," I mumble.

"Are you sure that Max was telling you the truth, Jen?"

"Look, I know we were only on a few dates, but I really liked him," I give her back the phone and go to rest my head back on my pillow, but a sharp pain runs through my neck, so I have to bring it back up. "If you would've seen his expression when he saw me tied to the pipe the first time and when he saw Phil on the floor when he came back... then you'd understand."

"But he closed the door on you, Jen," she's insisting. "He left you locked down there. I don't care what expressions were on his face. I don't care how much of a gentleman he was before that."

"I know that, but then why would he call 911 to help me?"

Michelle gets up from my bedside and puts her hands on her hips as she starts pacing in small circles near the door. "Are you sure there wasn't a neighbor around that might have heard you yelling or something?"

"I doubt it. I really thought it was you but when they said anonymous, Max was the only person I can think of. The closest neighbor from there is a mile away, so it's not likely anyone heard or saw anything. It sure as hell wasn't Phil either. He wasn't moving after I beat him with the shovel... It didn't look like he was breathing," I lower my voice back to a whisper as I look at her. "I really think I killed him. I'm serious."

"Then if he's dead, where could he be?" she whispers back.

"Wherever Max is?" I shrug.

"If he is dead, Jen," she pauses. "You realize that Max knows that you killed him? You don't think that's going to anger him? You don't think he's going to tell someone? Maybe that's why he left you locked in the basement that last time?"

I shrug again. "I'm not so sure of anything anymore. All I know is that I need more answers from Max and he's not here."

A moment passes when Michelle says, "So, you're telling me that this was all just a terrible coincidence? You just met Max twice, out of random... and then it just so happened that his brother," she pauses to hold up her fingers into air quotes, "accidentally crashed into you?"

I give her a know-it-all look. "Well, you did say it was fate."

She doesn't laugh or give me a sarcastic look back. Instead, she smirks at me. "I did say that."

"Coincidence or not, I still want to talk to Max," I say. "I don't think he knew that Phil was going to hurt me. I want to know where he was the whole time or where he is now... Something just doesn't add up."

"Max might not be so willing to talk to you, Jen... not after what you did to Phil. You realize that, right? Maybe that's why he called in as anonymous."

I have nothing to say but just shrug my shoulders because she might be right. I go to lean up to look at the phone but more pain shoots down my back. "Damnit," I wince.

"Woah, stay still. You should not be moving around so much. How long do you have to stay here?"

"I think I heard the doctor tell me that I have to stay until at least tomorrow to monitor me."

"You did tell him that you were in a coma not even a month ago, right?"

I nod. "Yeah. I got a head scan already and they told me I'm fine. Plus, it was in my medical history anyway."

"Well, what else did the cop say? How did she leave off

with you?"

"She just said that she was going to look for both Phil and Max. Then she asked me if I want to press charges against either of them, but I only said I'd press charges on Phil." I sigh. "Not that it probably will matter," I mutter.

Michelle presses her lips together. "Well, I'm staying here until you leave."

"No, you're not," I tell her.

"Jen..." She's giving me discerning eyes.

"I'll be fine. You have to go to work tomorrow morning and you left in the middle of it today. Your boss is probably going to fire you... that is, if you're not fired already. I'll be fine, trust me."

I can tell that she's contemplating on fighting with me when suddenly her eyes widen, and she leaps up from the bed abruptly which startles me.

"Holy shit! I have to go back to Stoney's!" she gasps.

"What? Why?"

"So, uh, I kind of told Luke that Max had you in danger and I forced him to give me his address. The cops pissed me off when they said they couldn't help me, so I just drove straight to Stoney's since that was the only thing that I knew about Max," she says as she rushes to grab her purse from the chair.

"Did you actually get Max's address from him?" I question.

"Oh, hell yeah I did! He was being an asshole, so I jumped over the counter and made him show me Max's file. I got his brother's name, phone number, and his address out of it. I called him first, but it went straight to voicemail, so I went to his apartment. I didn't know what his brother's name was, so I ended up getting it from his neighbor. That's how I found his social media. I saw that he worked in a bar in North Townshed and so I went there. There was only one bartender that was working, and the place was packed. I asked her if she knew where Phil's parent's house was in Townshed, but she had no idea, so I left then I ended up aimlessly driving around Townshed for a little bit. I was heading back to Forest when you called me. Then, I turned around and came straight here."

I have to blink a few times to think about what she just told me.

"What did you think I was doing this whole time?" She puts her hands on her hips. "I wasn't going to just sit at home or go back to work and wait a whole day for the police to start looking for you! I had to do something!"

I begin laughing hysterically as I picture her jumping the counter at Stoney's. "I wish I saw you jump over the counter in that dress and those heels," I say in between giggles.

"Okay, that morphine might be making you delusional right now," she shakes her head. "This isn't funny. We don't want Luke asking questions. You know how he is." She looks at me and sighs. "Damnit, I really don't want to leave you here alone."

"Michelle, go. I've worried you enough. I'm good now. Phil's gone and I'm safe here. I got what I wanted - to find the person who hit me."

"Yeah, you got him alright," she mumbles which makes me dryly chuckle, and I give her the phone number to my hospital room before she leaves.

When I am left alone in the room again, it takes a few minutes for me to allow what I went through to sink in. *I really just killed a man.* I'm not remorseful for what I did because I know I had to do it. *I had to defend myself...* I'm just not sure that I feel as good about it as I should. I am relieved that I broke free of the basement and survived that psychopath, but when I think about Max... a part of me feels bad. His parents died. His ex-girlfriend died and whatever the hell I was to him; new girlfriend or not, I'm the reason for his brother dying.

I didn't tell Officer Marien that Max hurt me because he really never did. However, I still don't know where he was during the whole time and why he left me locked in. A part of me wants it to stay that way; not knowing the true answer... but I know that the more persistent part of me is not going to let that happen. Not especially since my gut is telling me that he was the anonymous caller.

CHAPTER 21

Just when I thought the worst moments of my life happened, I'm back in the white room, *frozen on my back and I can't move my body again.* Even though I know why I am here this time, it doesn't make me feel any less uneasy because this just means that I must've gone back into a coma, but how is that possible?

I was wide awake after Michelle left the room. My head was killing me, but I was *fine.* My doctor told me I was fine too… and so did the nurse who came in to check on me a few minutes after Michelle left. That's the last thing I can remember before waking up here. *I bet I'm back here in this room because of Phil again.* I probably fell back into a coma once I fell asleep.

Fuck this, though! I'm not staying in this white room again. I refuse to.

As I am attempting to move my body, I begin to hear beeping sounds nearby. They were the same ones that I heard when I was coming out of my coma.

But I'm not awake right now… *or am I?*

I can't really tell. I still feel paralyzed to this bed, like I'm being restrained, and I can't lift my arms or my legs… but I hear the beeps.

Suddenly, I hear a door opening so I try to lift my head, but I can't see anything.

"Hello?" I call out hoping to hear a response, but I don't

get one.

I let time pass before I call out again. When I do, I feel the presence of a person to the right of me, so out of reaction I try to sit up… and to my surprise, it actually works this time. I'm distracted that I can move my body when the person that I heard open the door is suddenly rushing toward me, and I see that it's Phil.

I go to jump off the left side of the bed and run in the opposite direction of him, but he catches me by my hair, tugging me back onto the bed. I'm twisting and turning away while screaming for what seems like eternity until I hear a woman's voice say my name. Phil gets off me and I run toward the voice which I realize came from a nurse who is standing by the door.

"He's going to kill me!" I gasp as I rush over and into her arms.

"Jennifer," she says my name when she grabs hold of me and leads me into the hallway. I'm hyperventilating in front of her until I start to hear my name again.

"Jennifer, it's okay. It's okay…"

In a blink of an eye, I find myself gasping in a hospital bed.

"It's okay, Jennifer. Everything is okay. You are at Townshed Memorial hospital. You are safe," a female nurse is standing beside my bed, gently rubbing my forearm to calm me down.

I'm sitting up, but I don't remember doing that. I just remember Phil in the white room… and now I'm here. "I… I," I stutter as I take a second to realize what just happened. *I was never in the white room, and I didn't run out of this one. Phil isn't here either.* "I think I was having a nightmare."

"It's okay, dear. Just try to go back to sleep. Would you

like me to leave the door open or close it when I leave?"

"Uh, you can close it," I groan while I try to get comfortable in the bed. Before she closes the door, I catch a glimpse of the clock on the wall which reads two in the morning. I guess I only slept for a couple hours since Michelle left. I want to go back to sleep but I unfortunately have to use the bathroom. I say unfortunately because every part of my body hurts whenever I get out of bed and shuffle the few feet over to it in my room.

What would normally take me about two minutes to use the bathroom, it just took me a good five more because I'm literally moving like I am an eighty-year-old. That's how much pain I am in. As I am washing my hands in the sink, I look down at my bandaged forearms. The doctor said the paramedics treated my rope burns in fair time so I should heal within a few days. However, I wish that were the case for my bruised cheek. My cheek will probably take longer to heal but at least I will be able to cover it up with foundation and powder until then.

I'm going to have to dodge my parents for a little while as well. There's no way I'm going to be able to see them until I heal better. I can't let them know what happened and I never will. I don't think I need to tell them or worry them anyways. I won't even know where to begin. Michelle called me once she got home after leaving the hospital and we already devised a plan on what to tell my parents. She is going to text my mom when she wakes up to tell her that I lost my phone so that way she doesn't worry if she calls and it goes straight to voicemail, and that I will call her when I get a new one, which I plan to do as soon as I leave the hospital. Hopefully, my doctor will discharge me early enough, so I can make it to the store before it closes.

I just got back in bed and am beginning to shut my eyes when my door starts opening and the light from the hallway distracts me. It's probably a nurse coming to check my vitals since they've been coming in every half an hour or so throughout the night. I hear the door close as I am trying to go back to sleep, but that's odd to me because the nurses normally leave it open when they walk in. I start to sit up in the bed, feeling uneasy and in the next second, I'm suddenly reliving the same moment with Phil all over again.

He's rushing straight toward me, bandaged, limping and grunting... just like in my dream. *Unfortunately, this time I'm most definitely not dreaming.* I don't have time to yell for help before he's already climbing on the bed and on top of my body. Giving me no time to react, he's got his right hand over my mouth to keep me quiet, while his knees are pressing over both the bandages on my forearms. I try to twist my body away while I murmur small screams, but I can barely move. His body weight is *so heavy* on my bruises. I'm in a shitload of pain and he must be too because he's grimacing with every struggle.

Still, he's not letting the pain stop him. His knees are pressed down on my arms while he's struggling to keep his hand over my mouth. I think he's trying to use his left hand to pull the pillow out from under me... maybe to suffocate me, but I keep fidgeting so he can't succeed. Even though it aches to lift my lower body because of my herniated disc, I quickly thrust my hips up with him still on top of me. Phil is so much heavier than I am, but I continue to buck my hips up and down as many times as it takes until I can manage to make him slightly lose his balance.

His knees slide off my forearms just a bit which makes him let go of my mouth. He grabs hold of the bedside railing so he can steady himself. Right as his hands release my lips, I slide my body away quickly, then I reach over to my left side where my IV stand is, and I grab it and slam it right against his head. He tries to catch himself from falling off the bed, but I don't let that happen by assisting him with a push.

He lands on the floor, groaning and gasping for breath as he fumbles to stand back up.

But there's no way I'm going to let him. There's no fucking way I'm going to let this man live again.

Regardless of the searing pain in my arms, I lift the IV stand in the air and slam it down right onto his stomach *and I don't stop there.*

I lift the stand once more, and then I slam it down on top of his head. Finally, Phil is laying on the floor just like he was in the basement after I beat him with the shovel, but this time, I know he's actually dead.

CHAPTER 22

One week later

It's been exactly one week since I killed Phil and today is his funeral. I didn't plan to go to it, but I caught myself driving here when I was on my way to work this morning and I found myself parking a few feet away from his funeral service. I only know that it is today because I have been keeping tabs on his social media profile every day this past week. I saw a post in his tagged photos from one of his coworkers which said they raised money together to hold his funeral service.

I assume that the handful of people that are surrounding Phil's gravestone in the columbarium right now are those coworkers. I just counted five people. Unfortunately, none of them are Max. I haven't heard from him since he last left me in the basement and I'm starting to think I never will again. There's been no sign of him anywhere; not even on Phil's profile and no one has mentioned him. I thought that someone would have something to say but there's not one comment about him, not even under any of the older posts with photos of Max in them.

The police are not looking for him anymore either. Instead of searching for Max like Officer Marien had told me she would, she ended up closing my case the same night when I killed Phil. When she came back to the hospital after Phil attacked me, and saw him beaten on my hospital floor, I guess she realized that I clearly acted in self-defense because the tone in her voice changed from skeptical to believing toward me the second time around. So, thankfully, I didn't go to jail as I had begun to start mentally preparing myself for. Between my experience with Forest Hill's police and the disbelieving look in Officer Marien's face earlier to that, I thought that I was really going to get arrested for murder but thankfully, I didn't.

Before closing my case, Officer Marien told me that the house was listed under Phil's name and not under Max, so technically Max didn't need to be questioned anymore. Therefore, since I still chose to not press charges on Max, the police basically had no real reason to search for him. I have not heard anything from Officer Marien or anyone from Townshed police since then and I don't expect to either.

I was given a list of psychologists that my insurance covers, but I don't think I'm going to go see anyone. No matter who I chose out of the list, it's a forty-dollar copayment every visit and I just simply don't have any extra money to keep giving away right now. Between my nonexistent car that I'm still paying and all the hospital bills that I've occurred from my accident and after escaping the basement, I literally have ten dollars to my name right now. Besides, after everything I've been through the last thing that I want to do is talk to a strange doctor that I don't know because I can't even tell them everything that truly happened. *The only person that I really want to talk to about what happened is Max.*

Three days ago, I stopped at his apartment after hounding Michelle to give me his address, but he wasn't there. She was hesitant on giving it to me because she fears that Max wants to hurt me, but I convinced her to give it to me anyway. I even knocked on the nosey neighbor's door that Michelle had told me about, but the lady wasn't home, so I ended up leaving.

According to Michelle, Max hasn't been back to work at Stoney's yet either. After telling Luke that she was drunk and was being the overly protective friend that she is, he believed her. I mean, given her personality, I don't know why he wouldn't have. However, he did make sure to mention that he found it very suspicious that she came in there *hunting* for Max, and that Max was a no show for his shift the following day, (Luke's words exactly). I have not gone back to Stoney's yet and I don't plan to go until I heal a bit more. I only went to work twice this week and I caked my face in makeup to cover the bruises. To say that people made comments was an understatement.

Right now, I am sitting in the cemetery in front of a gravestone with the name Margie on it. I am about two hundred feet away from where Phil's funeral is taking place. I chose to sit here because I am trying to look inconspicuous, even though I don't really need to hide my appearance or worry about anyone noticing who I am from this far away or up close anyway.

A reporter from Townshed's news station came to the hospital shortly after the police came back after I killed Phil. I guess she tried to come into my room and question me, but I told the police to tell them that I did not want to share my story and to keep my name out of the media. To my surprise, they have obliged. I've been checking for new articles or updates but so far, I've only seen one article. It basically summed up that a young woman acted in self-defense when a man attacked her in her hospital room without mentioning any names. They also reported that the same man kept the woman captive for many hours prior to that and no more details are to be released about either person since the case is now closed.

So, no one should know that they were talking about me except for Michelle, the hospital staff... which I think was a total of six nurses, and one doctor on that floor, and Max, wherever he may be. He's definitely not anywhere in this cemetery that I can see of, so I should probably really leave now. The more I continue to think about him, I think I'm beginning to torture myself mentally. I still don't have any remorse about what I did to Phil, but I don't feel any better about it yet either. I never imagined that I would ever hurt anyone or anything in my life, let alone kill a person. I've never even been in a fist fight with anyone. But still, I always knew that if I had to defend myself, I would, and that time had come in the basement. I'm proud that I did defend myself but my sadness for Max still keeps a hold on me.

The fact that we went from having such a nice weekend to absolute hell within a matter of an hour eats away at me. I have all these open-ended questions for him, but I know that I need to start concentrating on getting my life back together again. Sitting here in this cemetery isn't helping that.

I get back into my car and turn on the engine to get ready to head to work. I got my beamer fixed two days ago thanks to Michelle. It cost a couple hundred to fix and she paid the whole thing, even though I didn't ask her for help, but she insisted and I'm grateful. Just as I am about to put my car in drive, my phone rings so I pull it out of my purse in the passenger seat beside me.

It's my mom. I've been trying to dodge her calls or just

get her off the phone as quickly as I can whenever I talk to her these past few days, but it's been difficult. I'm not trying to take anything out on her. I know that she cares and has no idea what I've really been through since my accident happened.

"Hi mom," I say in a perky voice as I close my eyes and rest my head back against the headrest. I am trying to mask how tired and drained I truly am.

"Good morning, dear. Are you excited for your first day of college this week? I can't believe it's only two more days away!"

I'm not excited one bit. I haven't even been thinking about it. The last time I spoke or even had a thought about college was with Max, when I freaked out after I saw the car accident.

"Yeah. I can't wait," I lie as I keep an eye on Phil's funeral from my driver seat.

"I haven't seen you in a while, sweetie. I miss you. Do you want to stop at the restaurant today for some lunch?" my mom asks, and I hesitate before answering. It's a miracle that I dodged my parents for a week already. My forearms are healed now and I'm able to cover up my bruises with my foundation but to be safe, I rather wait just a few more days to see my parents again. That way, I won't have to cake my face in makeup, which will most likely cause them to ask me questions about it because I barely ever wear makeup when I hang around them.

"Uh, no. I'm actually meeting Michelle for lunch," I pause to swallow as I'm still holding back my tears. "I'm sorry, mom. We can hang out this weekend."

"Oh, great! Why don't we go have dinner at Lucky Star's Friday night? We haven't been there in a long time! I've been thinking about their pizza for the past few days now.

Dad gets off work at 7:00 p.m. We can meet you there at 8:00 p.m."

I smile as I hear the excitement in my mom's voice. I must be doing a good job at holding back my emotions right now because my mom does not seem to notice. I exhale away from the phone before I speak. "I can't wait. Tell dad I said, hi. I'll talk to you later," I try to smile when I speak as I remember Max telling me the phrase - *over falsification of confidence is the key to sounding confident.*

"Okay, love you. Call me if you need anything," she says, always emphasizing the *call me* part.

I tell her that I love her back and end the call with tears streaming down my face. I'm crying uncontrollably and gasping for air. I'm a blubbering mess right now and I can barely control it. *Why did any of this have to happen to me? Why couldn't I just leave things alone? Why did it have to be Phil? And more importantly, why did it have to be Max?* I don't believe anyone is perfect, but I felt so unbelievably comfortable with Max. I know he was only the second guy that I've ever dated but I just can't forget about him so easily, not after everything that's happened.

And especially, not when I have so many unanswered questions.

—

I hear a knock on my front door right when I am just about to sit down on my couch and relax. I was going to ignore it, but the person just knocked again, so I decide to get up and go see who it is. I nearly pass out from shock when I look through the peephole.

It's Max. He's here in the hallway of my building, standing right in front of my door.

I swing it open, fighting back the urge to release tears

when his deep eyes immediately look down into mine.

"I missed you so much. I'm so sorry," he says through sobs which is making me tear up too.

"Where were you? Why did you leave me in the basement? Max, I..." I have too many questions swirling in my mind.

He steps toward me with his arms out to hug me and I can't help myself but fall right into him. *It's all I wanted... It's all I've been needing.* I nuzzle my head into his chest, letting him embrace me around the small of my back with his large hands. The trace of his fingertips running up my spine and to the nape of my neck gives me goosebumps. *I've missed his touch. I've missed it so much.*

Something beeps in the distance, distracting me from him so I let go and lift my head up to look up but he's not there anymore.

I'm suddenly gasping for breath in my bed, and I realize the beeping is the alarm clock going off on my phone. *I was dreaming about Max again.* Ever since I left the hospital, I've been having both nightmares about Phil and also dreams of Max. Most of the dreams have been replays of the few dates we went on or just us being together in general, but this dream was different this time. What I just dreamt never happened in real life. I just sort of wish it would.

Everything in the dream felt so real; the way he was waiting for me at the door... his touch on my skin when he held me. I didn't even realize that I was crying in my sleep until I just touched my face and felt the tears on my cheeks.

Even though I know that I shouldn't, I grab my phone from my nightstand to look at Phil's profile for any new tags or comments, but I don't see anything new that I haven't seen already. I should stay home and relax since it's my day off of work, but my mind isn't going to let me do that. I throw on a purple V-neck hoodie, a pair of jeans, and boots, then head out to my car.

Ten minutes later, I park my beamer into the parking lot of Max's apartment building. I know that Michelle fears Max will hurt me, but I honestly don't think he would. He knows where I live and where I work. If he wanted to inflict harm on me in anyway, well I believe that he would have done it by now, so I'm not scared of him.

I just have questions and I want my answers. I can't move on without getting them.

My heart races while I grow increasingly anxious as I approach his door. After two knocks, I take a step back and wait a few seconds. No one answers so I look down to the right and left of the hallway before I try to turn the doorknob. It's locked just like it was the last time I was here, so I turn around and knock on the nosey neighbor's door. This time the elderly woman that Michelle told me about is home.

"Can I help you?" She is wearing a red bathrobe and curlers are placed throughout her bright red hair.

"Hi. Sorry to interrupt you, ma'am," I say. "Um, I was looking for one of the guys that live here." I point to Max's door behind me. "His name is Max. I haven't heard from him in a few days and was just a little worried about him. I was wondering if you might've seen him lately?"

The woman puts her palms up to her cheeks as she sighs and shakes her head. "Oh no dear, I have not seen him." She gives me sad eyes. "Did you know his brother?"

I have to quietly swallow before I answer, "no, I did not."

"Oh, well I heard that his brother sadly passed away recently. I haven't seen Max, or anyone enter that apartment for at least a week now." She shakes her head again as she looks past me toward Max's door. "Oh, it's so sad. He seemed like a nice young man, that Phil. Max is a sweetheart too. I figured that he might be with family grieving. I don't know what happened to Phil, but it's such a shame to hear. He was so young."

If you only knew the real story.

"I hope Max comes back soon though," she continues. "Rent is due next week. If he's late, our landlord is going to raise hell. I've been living here for ten years. That man has no compassion for anyone. I've seen him evict tenants with the slightest reason. He is very money hungry. The minute he doesn't get his rent on time, I'd say Max will have about a week or so before he starts to really annoy him," she says as she shakes her head while looking at Max's door.

I look back at the door in hopes that Max is maybe watching through the peephole... or that he'll swing the door open right now but it does not happen. "Well, uh, alright... thanks anyway," I sigh and look at the door one last time before I get in the elevator to go back downstairs.

As I'm passing the mailboxes in the lobby, I stop to see if I can open the one with his apartment number on it, but it's locked. I wanted to see if he's been picking up his mail, but I can't tell unless I break the mailbox open and I'm not going to do that.

While I sit in my car in the parking lot, I think about how tomorrow night is my first college class and that I should be getting prepared for it today but here I am, not prepared at all and staring hopelessly at a man's apartment that I barely knew. To think that I was excited to begin college with Max makes me embarrassingly chuckle to myself. I think I was falling in love with him but maybe I was just blinded by his kindness and masculine personality that I may have mistaken it for genuineness.

But when I start to doubt myself, I think about the anonymous caller. It had to be Max... and I need to know why. If he left me in the basement on purpose, why would he call for the police to help me? He said that he didn't know Phil crashed into me but if that is true, then where is he now? And where was he when I was alone with Phil in the basement?

As I sit here and look at his building, I think about what his neighbor told me. If Max does not show back up at his own apartment here in Forest, he will get evicted, but I wonder... what is going to happen to the house in Townshed? It was in Phil's name but now he is dead. I would think that the house should probably go to Max... but what if Max never shows back up there either? Then what would happen to it?

I have no interest in going back to the Townshed house ever again but if Max is not here and he hasn't been back at Stoney's, the house is the only other place that I think he might be. If he went anywhere else, then I wouldn't know. He's never mentioned any other family or friends to me, so I guess this is my last shot.

Even though I'm dreading it, I drive out of the parking lot, then I take a left off Max's street and head toward the highway to get to Townshed.

CHAPTER 23

An hour and a panic attack later, I pull into the driveway of the house in Townshed but this time I don't get the same tranquil vibe that I got when I first arrived here with Max. A cold shiver almost runs through my skin instead. Max's SUV isn't here, and the garage door is closed but I park my car in front of it in the driveway. I get out to lift up the garage door but when I do, I don't see his SUV inside either. My heart skips a little when I do see the tailgate of a pickup truck until my eyes shift to the whole thing, and I realize that it's not the truck that hit me. I can tell because this one is a two-door red pickup, and it looks completely opposite from what the security cameras caught. This truck is in perfect condition, and it has a Townshed license plate too.

I haven't been focused on finding the pickup because my goal was to really just find out who was driving it. I was still curious about the truck that I originally found in my junkyard adventure though, so I did look up the VIN number the other day, but I wasted my time and $37.50. The truck was registered to a lady by the name of *Laura* and the tags expired in Forest Hill a year ago so that truck wasn't Phil's.

I leave the garage and walk across to knock on the front door of the house. No one answers so I go to open the door, but it's locked. I walk around to the backyard, hoping that the slider door is still unlocked as I remember leaving it, and it is.

Feeling on the edge of both anxious and hopeful, I step into the living room. The first thing that I notice is Phil's dried up blood stains on the cushions of the couch, followed by just a few more stains on the carpeted floor near the basement door in the kitchen.

I never saw any of this until now because I never went back into the house after escaping the basement. I was sitting on the front porch with the paramedics and cops, but I was so out of it that I never even turned around to look inside of the house.

No wonder why Officer Marien was looking at me in the way she was when she mentioned there was a lot of blood.

"Hello? Anyone in here?" I call out as I slowly walk further into the living room. I don't hear anything, so I ease my nerves and continue toward the spare bedroom. I poke my head through the doorway and see that the room is empty, so l leave and go into the master bedroom. When I flip the light switch on the wall, the light does not turn on, so I go into the bathroom to turn on the light in there, but it doesn't work either. I guess the power is turned off in the house which is not showing any good sign that Max has been here. There is only a bit of daylight shining from the backyard in between the closed blinds on the window in the bedroom, but it's enough for me to see that the room looks just like we left it.

My sliver of hope in Max being here is starting to vanish as I leave the room and walk into the kitchen. As I stand here, the thought of Max sliding behind me and making coffee while I made us food strikes my memory, bringing tears to my eyes. *How did everything turn so quickly? We came here for peace, and we ended up getting the complete opposite of it.* I direct my eyes to the basement door before I walk over and decide to turn the doorknob to open the door.

I poke my head through the doorway slowly and take only one step inside to look down at the basement, keeping half my body almost in the kitchen while I hold onto the door. Just like the bedroom and kitchen; the basement looks the same - another sign that Max hasn't been here. The boxes that I kicked over are still on the ground and the mess that arose from when I was fighting Phil, looks like it hasn't been touched. The window is still busted out from when I broke it with the shovel too.

I step back into the kitchen to see if there is anything that is heavy enough that could have been put against the door to hold it closed because I'm still unsure of how I got locked in the basement in the first place. The barstools under the counter would be the only thing close by, to put up against the door, so I pick one up to see if Phil or Max used it to block the door. It's not heavy at all. I just picked it up easily. If I can pick it up with no problem, then there's no way that they used it.

Nothing is making any sense. I know I was alone in the house when I got locked in initially because I saw Max leave to go to the store before I went in the shower. I even had time to finish showering and make two trips down into the basement before it happened. If Max locked me in initially, he would have had to been in the house when I was bringing the bags into the basement, but I don't see how that could have been because this house isn't big. I would've heard or noticed that he came back. And I saw Phil arriving... at least, I think I did. If Phil was in the house prior to that at any time, I really think I would have known it, just like I would have known if Max came back.

Keeping the basement door open from inside the kitchen, I turn the doorknob a few more times before I decide to close the door again and open it once more. I make sure to slam it as hard as I can when I close it because I'm starting to think that maybe the door might have locked on its own. I do recall closing it behind me after taking the bag down into the basement... but I'm not sure if I had closed it behind me the first time.

The doorknob is turning just fine from inside the kitchen so I guess I wouldn't know if it locks from the basement unless I go on that side and close it from there to see myself. I really don't want to go back down there, but the perseverance in me doesn't care about my emotions right now. I know that I won't be able to stop thinking about this door unless I put my theory to the test. The window is still busted open so I can crawl out that way if the door does lock anyway. It's not like I can actually get locked inside this time because I do have a way out. Plus, I have my phone, and no one is trying to hold me hostage right now... so in theory, I should be fine.

Stepping into the basement and ignoring my rising anxiety, I take a deep breath before shutting the door behind me. As soon as I shut it, I immediately go to open it, but the door doesn't budge. I just locked myself in here again which means that this door does lock on its own, like I had suspected. I should feel relieved that I have the answer to how I first got locked in, but I'm not relieved one bit because... that just means that Max did lock me in here on purpose when he left with Phil the last time. I'm sure he knows that this door locks by itself, so that's probably why he closed it when he left with Phil - to purposely leave me down here.

My mind is running, and my heart is starting to beat

EVERYTHING LED ME TO YOU

fast as I stand here at the top of the stairs. *I can't believe I really just came back down here.* I quickly rush down the steps without taking a second glance at the blood stains or the water pipe that I was attached to as I make my way to the window. I'm not staying down here any second longer than I need to. The ladder is still near the window, so I climb up and crawl through, stepping carefully over what is left of the broken glass on the ground. I begin to walk back to my car before I abruptly decide to turn around and go to the backyard. There hasn't been any sign that Max has been in the house but just in case, I'm going to go check in the back.

While I stand here on the porch, I picture Max and I sitting at the table during lunch. I wish I knew that it was going to be our last time together. I also wish I didn't leave my phone on the table when I got up to get my birth control because according to him, that's how all this started.

Then again, I can't blame myself for trusting him. I was comfortable with Max. I didn't even think twice about leaving my phone near him because I had nothing to hide. Jealousy was not an emotion that he showed so my instincts didn't tell me that he was the type to snoop through my phone. Thinking about it now though, if I saw an ex's name pop up on his phone screen only days after running into the person, well then maybe I would've been a little curious too.

I walk over to the slider door to look into the house, and I direct my eyes to the blood stains on the couch which makes my mind wander back to Phil. I still don't regret killing him, but a bit of sorrow does consume me when I think about Max. I know I had to do what I did. I had to defend myself, both in the basement and in the hospital.

If I didn't, it would have been me getting buried in that cemetery the other day instead of him, and I have to keep remembering that. I think that's the only way I can try to make peace of this whole situation.

Peace. I stifle a small chuckle out loud when I think of the word. Ironically, the last time I really felt truly peaceful was with Max out here on this porch... and in the woods. I was a little nervous about hiking but then I was so grateful he took me. It was nice to be away from everything. It was a change that I didn't even know I needed. I felt so calm with him out there and he did too. I could tell by the way he conducted himself as he led me on the hike. It was like he was more comfortable out in the woods than in his house.

I turn to look at the woods. From the moment I woke up from my coma, I've been on a whirl wind of emotions, and I'm sick of it. Being out there in the woods with Max was the last time that I felt genuinely happy, and I want to feel that way again... but I'm starting to fear that I might not get that type of feeling back. Never in my life had I ever had a single thought about hiking in the woods or sleeping outside, let alone in a tent, before I met Max, but I was so glad I did it.

The tent. My eyes suddenly go wide when I think about camping. We never took down the tent after we woke up the morning of when everything happened, and I don't see the orange color of it popping through the trees. Even though Max set the tent up in the woods, he put it only a few feet past the tree line. He did it purposely, so I could still see it when I went to use the bathroom in the house throughout the night. I don't see the tent from the porch right now though.

Without even thinking twice, I find myself walking

toward the woods. With every step that I get closer to the tree line, and I don't see the tent, goosebumps rise on my skin. Once I am approaching closer. I confirm that it is gone, so I continue to walk in the same way that Max first led me on our hike. I don't know if he's out here, but I might as well try to find out.

CHAPTER 24

I've been walking in the same direction through the woods of where Max first took me for about fifteen minutes until just now because I needed to stop and take a breath. I am trying to take in the nature like I did on our hike before, but it feels different to be out here alone. When I was with Max, it felt better. Although I was paranoid about running into a bear on the hike, I still felt a sense of calmness with him, but I don't feel that way right now. My paranoia is heightened and I'm starting to second guess coming out here alone.

My thoughts shift when I suddenly hear something, and I quickly turn my head around toward the noise. Max and I didn't encounter any bears on our hike but knowing my luck recently, I wouldn't be surprised if one pops up on me right now. I stand here for a moment to listen for the noise again, but I don't hear anything anymore.

It's probably a tree branch or something and I'm just being paranoid again…

Or it really is a bear which means death is finally about to win against me.

Either way instead of turning around, I bravely continue walking. I don't know where all this bravery has come out of me lately because I never imagined doing the things I've done over these past weeks. From questioning people that I don't know, to getting detained by the cops, and breaking into a junkyard… I'm starting to wonder if the coma actually messed up my brain more than I was told, because I would have never done any of those things before the accident happened.

I continue walking when I see the same orange tent that Max and I camped in. It is set up a few feet in front of me. Before I can even walk toward it, I hear Max's voice to my right. "Jen?"

"M--Max?" I stutter when I see him. My sneakers feel like their stuck in quicksand. He's standing a few feet ahead of me to the right of the tent. His goatee has grown about half an inch, and he doesn't have a buzzcut anymore. He's also not wearing the same clothes that I remember last seeing him in. Now he's wearing a pair of cargo pants and an unbuttoned long sleeve flannel shirt, which reveals a plain black long sleeve under it.

"How did you know I was here?" he asks with pressed eyes.

"I… I came to look for you inside of the house," I stutter, "I noticed the tent was gone when I was in the backyard… and I didn't remember us taking it down, so I came out here." I look over at the tent, then back to him. "You've been out here this whole time?"

He nods his head yes, then looks down toward his boots. I don't know what else to say. I can only keep exchanging my glance from him and to the tent. I hoped that he would be here but an equal part of me didn't think I'd actually see him. It was more hope than anything, so I feel both relieved and nervous right now. He's projecting the same body language toward me, just as he had the first time of when he saw me in the basement tied to the pipe.

Silence passes between us for a few more seconds

before Max speaks. "Can we sit down so I can explain everything to you, Jen?"

I mumble a form of yes, then I walk slowly over to the tent to sit down on the log outside of it. A cooler sits on the floor next to it which is open, and I can see a few bottles of water and some snacks inside. The cooler is not the same one that Phil slid in front of me in the basement but the presence of it makes me think back to when I was being held captive. I look away, forcing those memories out of my head, and I sit down on top of the log.

Max waits for me to sit down before he goes to sit on the ground just a few feet in front of me. His eyes are bloodshot, and there are dark circles under them.

"First, I want you to know that I never intended for you to get hurt," he says as he rests his elbows on his knees. "I didn't know that Phil was going to do what he did to you, Jen. I really didn't," he pauses. "I should have never called him, and I should not have gone through your phone to begin with. When I saw my truck in your text--"

"What? It was your truck?" I gasp. "You-- you were there that night? You told me it was Phil-"

"No, no, no, shit!" he urgently interrupts me while he shakes his head. "That came out wrong!" he sighs. "Yes. It was my truck, but Phil was driving it. He took it to work and crashed into you on the way home from his shift that night. I wasn't with him. His license was suspended from a DUI, and his truck was broken so he would always take mine," Max pauses and lets out a deep sigh. "Phil was drunk when he crashed into you. He was already on probation from previous DUI's which is why he drove away after he hit you that night. That's why," Max exhales again, "he did what he did to you at the house." His eyes meet mine, but I release our gaze and shake my head.

"So-- so, you're telling me that Phil assaulted me and held me hostage because he didn't want to go back to jail? Are you serious? That doesn't make anything right at all!" I shout as I can't believe what I'm beginning to hear.

"I know that! I completely agree with you!" Max quickly says, bringing his eyes back to mine. "Please, just let me finish. This is really hard for me to explain. I didn't think you ever wanted to see me again…"

I wanted my answers. I know that I need to listen to them whether I like what they are or not, so I silently nod my head for him to go on.

"Phil bartended on the other side of town. He would always drink on the job and would come home drunk a lot," Max says as he rolls his eyes, "which is how he got a few DUI's and why he was on probation from them. He had a bit of an alcohol problem and I hated it, but he would never listen to me. If I hid my keys from him, he would just find a way to jump or hotwire my truck. I knew he took it to work the night he crashed into you, but I didn't know that he got into an accident until the next day," He looks back down at his shoes as his eyes are becoming glossy with tears. "Phil told me he hit a tree on the ride home, so I didn't know that he actually crashed into someone… especially that it was you. I only figured it out when I looked at your phone… and I'm sorry for doing that. I should have never snooped. I guess I got insecure or whatever when I saw that Nate texted you after he called," Max sighs. "When I looked at the message, I noticed the thumbnail photo of a truck in the text under it, so I clicked on it because it looked like my pickup. I called Phil when I went to the store and made him tell me the truth, then he hung up on me," he exhales and wipes away the few tears that have snuck out of his eyes. "When

I came back, he was sitting on the couch, but I had no idea that he was going to show up. I didn't know that he had such terrible intentions. He said he was opening the door in the basement for you, but you fell back-"

"Woah!" I gasp as I cut his words off, but he stops me from continuing to speak.

"*But I know you didn't fall, Jen!* I know he pushed you and I'm *incredibly* sorry... I know my apologies aren't going to help but I didn't know that he'd hurt you. I honestly didn't," he pauses. "I went to go down to the basement to check on you, but Phil got in front of me first and then... that's when I saw you down there. I- I was stunned. I-"

"Then why didn't you fight Phil when you saw me?" I look at him with questionable eyes when I interrupt him again. "You said you wanted to untie me, but you didn't try very hard."

"I really wanted to, believe me I did," he pauses, "but Phil's not himself when he drinks. He's an angry drunk and by the time I got there he was already a few beers in," he sighs. "I guess he freaked out when I told him that someone caught him on camera and I-- I don't know..." he shakes his head again. "Everything escalated so quickly, I didn't know what to do. I'm sorry that I didn't fight him... I really am. I guess, I'm just used to letting him always control everything," he sighs. "But I'm not using that as an excuse at all." Max's demeanor isn't showing any signs of anger or malice directed toward me but more so to himself when he speaks.

So, Phil was drunk when he hit me. That's not surprising. Not by what I smelt off him every time he came near me in the basement.

"Max, where were you during the whole time I was

EVERYTHING LED ME TO YOU

down in the basement then?" I ask while I cross my arms against my torso.

His shoulders drop. He doesn't directly look at me and says in such a low tone that I think I hear him wrong, "I was looking for Michelle."

"Wh--what?" I blink my eyes a few times in confusion as my eyebrows raise. "Looking for Michelle? Why? What were you planning on doing to her?"

"Nothing, I swear!" he says quickly. "Phil got in my head and freaked me out after she called you. He told me to go look for her since she probably thought that I had you in danger," he sighs, "which I did. And again, *I'm so sorry.* I wanted to go back downstairs to help you, but Phil was blocking the door," he exhales and looks me right in the eyes. "I figured that I'd leave and look for her so that I could explain everything and I... I don't know," he pauses. "I didn't really have a plan, but I was *never* going to hurt her, I swear. I went to my apartment, then I drove by your place but that was it. I realized that I made a mistake in leaving you, so I drove back here." He breaks eye contact from me when he continues, "Then I came back here and that's when I went down to the basement and saw Phil on the floor. I wanted to come back for you after I dropped him off at the hospital," he pauses to close his eyes and exhales, "but I found out that Phil was the reason my ex-girlfriend died and I just... I couldn't come back to face you. I didn't know how to explain everything."

I look at him confused as I think about what I saw on Monica's profile. "Wait, are you talking about Monica?"

Max presses his eyebrows together. "How do you know about her?"

"Michelle found her on Phil's profile. I thought she committed-"

"Suicide," he finishes my sentence and nods his head. "She did. She overdosed on some pills that Phil gave her," he pauses. "But I didn't know that until I was taking him to the hospital. He told me to look at his phone before I dropped him off and I found the texts between them. I still have it," he says while he gestures toward the tent. "I can show you. All I have to do is charge it. He was trying to get with her the whole time that me and her were together. He was encouraging her to leave me," Max sighs, "and he was also encouraging her to kill herself. She was going through depression. I didn't know that it was so bad, but I guess Phil did. She was confiding in him, but he was also manipulating her, and she didn't even know. I had no idea either. I didn't know how to explain all of this to you after I dropped him off, and I didn't think you would listen to anything I would say anyway. So, I made an anonymous call to 911 and told them that you were trapped in the basement and needed medical care. I gave them the address, then hung up. It was the only thing that I could think to do. I just wanted you to get back to safety. I should have never left you alone with Phil."

I am appalled at everything Max just told me. My mouth is dropped open and I can't form any words into a response. I wanted answers but it's just *so much* to wrap my head around right now. I wanted to see him, but I wasn't prepared for this conversation at all. I didn't expect to hear anything even remotely close to what he's telling me... especially about Phil. The quietness in the air takes over us as I think about everything. Max seems genuinely sorry right now... but if he's so sorry, then why did he leave me locked in the basement?

"Why did you close the door on me when you left with Phil, then? I went back in the basement before I came out here to look for you. I know it locks on its own. Why did you close it on me?"

Max's eyes grow wide before he lets out a very slight chuckle which makes me scrunch my forehead. "You really are Nancy Drew," he mumbles under his breath. I go to speak but he does instead. "Jen, I didn't mean to leave you locked in there. I just closed the door behind me without thinking about it. I was panicking when I was carrying Phil up the steps. I thought he was dead... I didn't even realize that I shut the door on you until I was dropping him off at the hospital. It was an accident. That door has had that lock problem for years now. It gets jammed and automatically locks when you close it. The only way to open it is from the kitchen or if you knew where the key is inside the basement. That was part of the list of things that we needed to fix before we were going to Airbnb the house." He connects his eyes with mine again, then scrunches his forehead. "What made you go into the basement to check the lock? That means you had to have locked yourself in there again to know that."

"I didn't understand how I got locked down there in the first place," I shrug. "I just needed to figure it out myself. I saw that the window was still broken, so I knew I had a way out," I pause, then I mumble, "it's not like I didn't have experience doing it before."

Max presses his lips together. "I wasn't lying when I said that you are a strong person."

Silence passes between us as I let everything run through my mind. Max's demeanor is making it hard for me to doubt him in the moment. The calm collective guy that I met weeks ago is now the complete opposite. In the short amount of time that I did get to know him, I never imagined him to look at me this way - so vulnerable and defeated. I'm not blind to him being human and having those emotions... but it's just so unexpectedly overwhelming to see this side of him. I didn't expect to hear any of this but then again, I don't know what I was expecting. Max said he *thought* Phil was dead... but does he know what happened after he dropped him off?

"Max," I hesitate, unsure of how he is going to react. "Do you know what happened with Phil after you dropped him off at the hospital?"

"Mhmm," he mumbles softly. "I saw the news before I turned my phone off a few days ago. Even without mentioning your names, I knew they were talking about you guys. I'm so sorry that you had to do what you did."

"You're sorry?" I drop my head and scrunch my forehead as I blink a few times. "Max, *I'm sorry*. I-- I killed your brother. I'm surprised you're even speaking to me right now," I shake my head. "Michelle was terrified that you were going to hurt me if I ever saw you again."

Max's solemn expression turns into a look of sincerity. "Jen, I never wanted to hurt you and I still don't. I never will. I don't blame you for doing what you did to Phil. He was the only part of my family that I had left but," he exhales, "he always had his problems, even before our parents died. There have been so many times that he fucked things up for me in my life; but even though he was my brother, I can't forgive what he did to either you or to Monica. There's just no moral reason for any of his actions."

Tears are falling down my cheeks. I don't understand how any of this is happening right now. I don't understand how Max is only a few feet away, apologizing *to me*.

"You shouldn't have gone through what you did with

Phil. I should have never put you through any of that. I'll go turn myself in to the police. I shouldn't have run off out here. I just didn't know what to do," Max says.

"What? No, you don't have to do that," I wipe away my tears. "The police aren't looking for you. I didn't press any charges on you. I told them that you didn't hurt me."

"You didn't have to do that," he mumbles.

"Well, you never did," I say softly.

"It was my fault that you got kidnapped and beaten up by my own brother. Everything that happened to you was my fault."

"Phil crashing into me wasn't your fault, Max," I say.

"It was my truck that he was driving that night," he sighs.

I look at the tent, then I direct my attention back to Max. By the looks of what is inside and around the tent, it seems like Max has been doing just fine on his own. "Were you just going to camp out here for the rest of your life?" I ask curiously.

"I didn't really have a plan," Max shrugs. "Everyone in my life is gone and I had nowhere to go. I don't have any other family so the only place I could think to go was out here. I didn't want anyone to find me, and I just wanted peace. I went into the house once to get a few things to camp out here but that's it." He looks around us before he lets a tiny grin appear on his face for only a second when he says, "I can't believe you came out here by yourself. I thought I was hallucinating when I saw you."

"I can't believe it either," I shake my head. "When I noticed that the tent was gone, I just followed my instincts. I went to your apartment twice but when your neighbor said that she hadn't seen you, I didn't know where else to look for you except the house. I didn't want to come back, but I needed to find you," I pause. "I had questions and you were the only person who could answer them."

"I kind of figured that you would eventually find me," he says. "You never gave up on finding my truck."

I dryly stifle a laugh at his comment and then I realize that I still don't know where the truck is. After everything Max just told me, I got distracted and didn't even get to ask the first question that started all this. "Wait, where is the truck? What did Phil do with it?"

Max's face tenses before he says, "It's here. It's in the woods. Phil parked it only a few feet further behind us. He hid it out here the same night of the accident and told me the next day."

My mouth falls open and my eyes get wide. Once again, I don't have any words. The whole time I had been investigating, and the truck was right here. I was so close to it for almost a whole weekend, and I had no idea even when I was out here with Max on the hike.

"Max." I raise my eyebrows while I think about the excuse that he said Phil gave him. "If Phil told you that he hit a tree, then why did you think it was normal for him to hide it out here?"

"That's a good question," Max answers with a tone of defeat. "I'm an idiot. I just believed what he said like I always have. I knew he was drunk but I honestly didn't think he hurt anyone… especially you. I just figured that it was probably best to leave it out here since it would cost the same amount of money to buy a new one. The truck was paid off anyway, so I didn't really think about it and got my SUV the next day. I don't know why I didn't question him putting it out here. Thinking about it after everything, it doesn't make sense at all… I know."

The slight sounds of the leaves in the wind, along with the birds chirping, both mask the silence between us for a moment before, I finally say, "I need to see it."

CHAPTER 25

After about ten minutes of following Max into the woods, we arrive in front of the pickup truck that I had been so desperate to find all this time. Just like what I found on the security cameras from the store and at the two houses on Burr, I'm standing in front of a four-door dark blue F-150 pickup truck with a dented inward hood, and a left busted headlight in front of me. The truck is parked right next to Max's SUV.

"Why is your SUV out here with it?" I question as I look back at Max who is standing not far behind me.

"I really thought the police were looking for me since I was sort of an accessory to kidnapping, so I drove it out here," he says in an ashamed like tone. "I didn't want it to be seen at the house." He looks past me at the truck and shakes his head. "I don't know what I was thinking. I'm an idiot for believing that Phil hit a tree. I just took his word for it."

He doesn't say anything but just shrugs his shoulders. I turn back around to look at the truck, then I start to walk around it, examining the hood and around to the bed of the pickup. I was so determined to find this thing and now I am in arms reach of it. The window on the passenger side is shattered, so I step up on the step to look through it. The airbags are deployed just like the ones in my scion were. Glass is all over the passenger seat and scattered onto the floor.

As I glare at it, I'm surprised that I still don't remember anything new from my accident. I thought that maybe something would jog my memory if I ever did see the vehicle that hit me again, but nothing comes to mind.

"How the hell did this thing make it all the way out here after totaling my car that night?" I mumble under my breath and Max hears me.

"That's a great question," he mutters.

I step off the truck and take a few steps back to stare at it some more when I think about what I went through in looking for this thing.

"Are… are you okay?" Max asks and I realize that I am chuckling out loud.

I turn around to see him staring at me with a look of worry but also uncertainty in his eyes. "I don't mean to laugh," I shake my head. "But you have no idea what I went through when I was looking for your truck. I literally got thrown in a jail cell for yelling at a cop and that was before I broke into a junkyard and got chased out by the owner and his dog too," I sigh as I shake my head.

A grin appears on Max's face again. "I told you that you are a strong person." His face turns solemn. "I'm so sorry for everything you went through, Jen. I really am. If I could go back and change things, I really would."

If Max is lying about any of what he just told me, I wouldn't know why. When it comes to Phil, I know Max is telling me the truth about Phil working at a bar since I saw it on his profile and the fact that he was a drunk because I witnessed that myself. Max also admitted to being the anonymous caller before I even got a chance to ask him about that first. He clearly didn't expect to see me again, so if all this was a lie… well then, he's damn good at improv.

"Like you said," I pause, "I don't think any more apologies between us are going to make up for everything that's happened," I say softly.

The undisturbed stillness in the air circulates heavily around us with only whisps of the tree branches and the sounds of the birds as we stand here. Unknowingly, I start to smirk again when I think about Michelle telling me it was fate that I met Max.

"Why are you smirking now?" Max's confusion in his face is back.

"Michelle swore us meeting was fate," I roll my eyes and sigh. "I don't think this is the definition of fate though."

"Maybe some sort of twisted fate," he mumbles.

"You did say everything happens for a reason," I press my lips, not meaning to sound so sarcastic. To my surprise he lets out a genuine laugh. "I told you I hate that saying," he pauses, "but I didn't say that it wasn't true. Jen, I really thought you would never want to see me again. You have every right to hate me."

"I don't hate you, Max. I knew that you were the anonymous caller, so my instincts told me there was more that I needed to know from you."

"I'm really glad I got to see you again. I've missed you," he says in a lower voice, almost sounding like he was afraid to say it.

"I missed you too, Max. I don't blame you for anything that happened. None of this was your fault." I look around the woods then back to him. "Since the cops aren't looking for you, you know that you can come back to Forest Hill, right? You can't live out here in a tent forever."

"I can't go back to my apartment." He looks down to his feet. "Too many memories with Phil."

He's right. Why would Max want to go back there? I sure as hell wouldn't. He will be constantly surrounded by memories of Phil if he does. I guess coming out here in the woods really was the best option for him.

"But I guess I can look for a new apartment," he says as he looks from his feet, then up to me.

"I think you should," I agree. "You were so ready to start college, Max. Our first day is tomorrow. You can't let everything that's happened stop you from doing what you planned."

"You should know," Max presses his lips into a half grin which makes me do so too. He looks around us then exhales deeply. "It would be really awesome to live out here forever, but I know it's not realistic for me. I know I have to go back to Forest Hill. I have to go back to my life."

"Max," I hesitate, "where do we go from here?"

"It's up to you," he shrugs. "I know you say you don't blame me, but I still blame myself… and I'm not sure if or how long it will take for me to get past it. If I can go back in time and fix everything, I really would," he hesitates, "but I want you to know that these past few weeks have sucked without you. I haven't been able to get you off my mind."

I let silence pass between us for another minute more before I go on to speak. I don't know how we are going to be together after this, but he says it's up to me and right now, I just know that I don't want to walk away from him.

"I know that life is not going to be easy after what we went through," I pause, "but I do know that I don't want to go another day without you."

As soon as I finish my sentence, Max is already stepping toward me to wrap his arms over my shoulders in a hug. Suddenly, in the next moment, just like in my dream,

I have my arms wrapped around his waist and I'm instantly crying. I can feel him crying against me, our bodies shaking. "I don't want to go another day without you either," he says as he looks down at me and he wipes the tears off my cheeks.

"I think we might need each other anyway," I say. "I haven't spoken to anyone about what happened. Well, besides Michelle. She's the only one who knows but still…" my voice trails off as I don't really know how to approach talking about Phil. Even though I wanted him to pay for crashing into me, I never wanted to kill him. Whoever it was, I didn't want the person to actually get physically hurt. I just wanted them to face some consequences for hitting me and driving away… but not in the way it happened. The moments of killing him in the hospital replay in my mind which makes me start crying again. I'm gasping and tears are falling down my cheeks. "I didn't want to kill him," I say in between sniffles.

"I know you didn't. You had to defend yourself and that's what you did," he whispers while he kisses the top of my head. "I just don't want to lose you too."

I look up at Max with teary eyes. "I don't want to lose you either."

Finally, it feels like a weight has been lifted off my chest and it's not because I got all my answers. It's because I'm with Max. I will never understand why the universe chose to lead us together in the way it did, but I am not going to fight it. In a twist of fate, everything ended up leading me to him.

ABOUT THE AUTHOR

Sara Kate

 Sara Kate started her writing career as a scriptwriter for promotional videos and short films. Years later, she wrote her first mystery novel and continues to write full-time in her RV. Aside from writing, she enjoys rollerblading, photography, painting, and anything thriller/mystery related.

https://www.sarakateauthor.com
https://www.instagram.com/sarakateauthor/
https://www.goodreads.com/sarakateauthor
https://www.bookbub.com/sarakateauthor
https://www.pinterest.com/sarakateauthor/sara-kates-books/

BOOKS BY THIS AUTHOR

Zoey's Memory

There must be a mistake. This must be a misunderstanding.

After being committed to a psych ward one morning, Zoey awakens hours later without the memory of actually arriving. She can't really recall anything that happened the day before either.

The Doctor won't release her until she believes that Zoey is not a danger to herself or anyone else but Zoey swears that this is all a mistake. Now Zoey is on a mission to pick up the pieces of the hours before arriving and soon she finds that in order to do so, she has to face her past family trauma years later.

Zoey's Memory is a light mystery about mental health, anxiety, and grief.

He Thought I Was His

It began with a late-night knock on her door. Then stranger events started to occur.

When Brynn realizes she is being stalked, no one comes to mind as a suspect.
But as her safety becomes threatened, her anxiety heightens.

Without a name to look into, the police aren't able to open an investigation, causing Brynn to become uneasy everywhere, including her own home. But just as her suspicions arise, her stalker sets his long-awaited plan in motion, and Brynn is left to escape a dangerous future she never saw coming.

He was always a step ahead of her. Even when she was looking right at him.

Everything Led Me To You

Jen moved into her first apartment and is ready to enroll in college until her plans get unexpectedly stripped away when she ends up in a coma for one week.

Upon awakening, she learns the cause of her injuries came from a hit-and-run car accident and the police have no leads as to who the driver could be. Without a clear recollection of what the vehicle looked like, Jen isn't of much help either.

When enough time goes by, the case gets closed, and Jen becomes infuriated. Her frustration feeds into persistence, leading her to do an investigation of her own. In a suburban city outside of Chicago, Jen believes someone must have heard or seen something that night.

Jen only wanted to find the other driver. She just didn't expect to end up on a dangerous and unsuspecting path to the answer.

Made in the USA
Monee, IL
09 October 2022

15532132R00144